In *Raindance Autumn*, Rusty Watt—the sweet-talking, fast-dancing cowboy introduced in *Return to Raindance*— is back, and he's ready to charm his way into your heart....

"You had me fooled,"

Annelise said. "I thought you were a gentleman."

"You don't wa̶̶̶̶̶̶̶̶ to be ̶̶̶̶̶̶ love ̶̶ by ̶̶ ̶̶ntleman. What you need ̶̶̶̶̶̶̶̶̶̶̶̶̶̶̶̶̶̶̶̶̶̶̶̶̶̶̶̶̶̶ ̶̶̶̶̶̶̶̶ fire," Rusty sa̶̶̶̶̶̶̶̶̶̶̶̶̶̶̶̶̶̶̶̶̶̶̶̶̶̶̶̶̶̶̶̶̶̶̶̶̶̶̶ms.

Annelise starte̶̶̶̶̶̶̶̶̶̶̶̶̶̶̶̶̶̶̶̶̶̶̶̶̶̶̶̶̶̶̶̶̶̶̶̶̶̶̶, he lowered his m̶̶̶̶̶̶̶̶̶̶̶̶̶̶̶̶̶̶̶̶̶̶̶̶̶̶̶̶̶̶̶̶̶̶̶̶̶̶̶ first time all over again—the awakening ̶̶̶̶ ̶̶ ̶̶̶̶ned her whole body. All thought of resistance fled as her arms went around him and her lips yielded to his. She shivered, and as she pressed even closer, he dragged his mouth from hers.

"Annelise!" It was little more than a ragged whisper. "My God, what are you doing to me?"

She swallowed in an effort to dampen her dry mouth. "I believe you were showing me how a real man kisses."

Dear Reader:

The spirit of the Silhouette Romance Homecoming Celebration lives on as each month we bring you six books by continuing stars!

And there are some wonderful stories in the stars for you. In the coming months, we're publishing romances by many of your favorite authors such as Sondra Stanford, Annette Broadrick and Brittany Young. In addition, we have some very special events planned for the summer of 1988.

In June, watch for the first book in Diana Palmer's exciting new trilogy, Long, Tall Texans. The initial title, *Calhoun*, will be followed later by *Justin* and *Tyler*. All three books are designed to capture your heart.

Also in June is Phyllis Halldorson's *Raindance Autumn*, the second book of this wonderful author's Raindance Duo. Don't miss this exciting sequel!

Your response to these authors and other authors of Silhouette Romances has served as a touchstone for us, and we're pleased to bring you more books with Silhouette's distinctive medley of charm, wit and—above all—*romance*.

I hope you enjoy this book and the many stories to come. Come home to Silhouette—for always!

Sincerely,

Tara Hughes
Senior Editor
Silhouette Books

PHYLLIS HALLDORSON

Raindance Autumn

Silhouette Romance

Published by Silhouette Books New York

America's Publisher of Contemporary Romance

For Doris Kelly Hall,
who would still be my favorite sister
even if I had others

SILHOUETTE BOOKS
300 E. 42nd St., New York, N.Y. 10017

ISBN: 0-373-08584-2

First Silhouette Books printing June 1988

PHYLLIS HALLDORSON,

like all her heroines, is as in love with her husband today as on the day they met. It is because she has known so much love in her own life that her characters seem to come alive as they, too, discover the joys of romance.

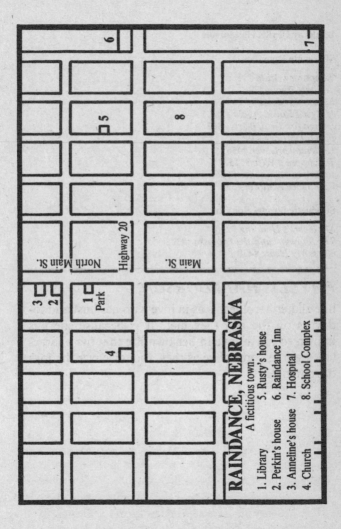

RAINDANCE, NEBRASKA
A fictitious town.

1. Library
2. Perkin's house
3. Anneline's house
4. Church
5. Rusty's house
6. Raindance Inn
7. Hospital
8. School Complex

Highway 20

North Main St.

Main St.

Park

Chapter One

Annelise Kelsey jerked her dangerously drowsy body to attention just in time to pull her ancient Plymouth Horizon back into her own lane before it had drifted more than a few inches across the white line. Beads of sweat broke out on her forehead and her heart started to pound as she realized how fortunate she was that there was practically no traffic on this narrow two-lane highway in northwestern Nebraska.

Thank heavens the sign a few miles back had read Raindance—30 Miles. She turned off the heater and rolled down the window to let the chilly late October night air blow against her face.

What was the matter with her? She'd felt fine when she'd hugged her mother goodbye in Kansas City at seven o'clock that morning. Actually, she'd been relieved to finally be starting the trip that would take her to her new position as librarian at the regional library in small, rural Raindance. Even though it wasn't her first choice in terms of either job or location, she felt free for the first time in her life.

It wasn't until a couple of hours after she'd stopped for lunch in Omaha that she'd begun to feel drowsy and a little disoriented. She doubted that it was anything she'd eaten. Her thick cream of broccoli soup had been fresh and hot, and the toasted bacon, lettuce and tomato sandwich had been served without mayonnaise. The coffee had been strong enough that it should have kept her awake even if she hadn't had a good night's sleep—which she had.

A wave of dizziness blurred her vision, and she shook her head to dislodge it. Maybe she was coming down with something. Darn. She couldn't get sick just as she was starting her career in a new and strange part of the country. Besides, usually she positively bloomed with good health. She hadn't missed one college class in the last four years because of illness.

She became aware of lights shining into the car from behind, and a glance in the rearview mirror confirmed the source. A big, heavy truck was tailing her with its lights on high beam.

Even with the window open the drowsiness returned, and Annelise took a deep breath of the brisk air. This was ridiculous. It's true she'd been driving pretty steadily all day, but she'd stopped and taken several breaks. As the lights of another small town loomed ahead she wondered if, for her own safety, she should stop there and not try to go on until morning. Unfortunately, the only motel she saw looked so run-down and dirty that it made her nauseated just thinking what the rooms must be like.

She drove on through the town, and when she was again in the dark she saw the truck, still close behind her, start to pull out into the oncoming lane.

While she watched, another sharp attack of dizziness rocked her, and everything went dark.

At first she was only aware of the pain. It seemed to surround and engulf her as though her body were wrapped in it. Gradually she realized someone was moaning. Then she heard another voice, deep and masculine. It was very close, but the words didn't seem to focus; they were just sound without meaning. She sank back into the soft, black cushion of nothingness.

When she surfaced again the pain and the voice were still there, but now she was lying on something hard, and someone was probing at her with large but gentle hands. They roamed impersonally over her arms, legs, ribs and shoulders, but when they touched her head the agony escalated and she cried out and opened her eyes.

It was almost as dark with her eyes open as it had been with them closed, except for a beam of light that was beside the figure bending over her. The hand moved to caress the back of her neck, and this time the man's words were firm and clear. "So you're finally with me. Sorry if I hurt you. Can you tell me what hurts the most?"

She could only see him in outline, but he looked huge. He was kneeling beside her, and she realized that she was lying on the ground with a blanket wrapped around her. Where was she, and how had she gotten there?

She heard another moan, but this time she felt it in her throat. Was she the one who'd been moaning before? She tried to lift her hand, but although her fingers moved she didn't have the strength to raise it.

"Ma'am, can you hear me? Where do you hurt?" He sounded insistent, but concerned.

"My—my head." Her voice was shaky and thin. "All—all over, but my head . . ."

Very carefully he ran his hands over her skull. They were caring hands, hands that would heal, not damage. She knew this with a certainty that defied logic. She could trust this gentle giant with her life. She closed her eyes and again sank into the peaceful darkness.

The third time she surfaced it was to a babble of voices and the continuing pain. She opened her eyes, afraid the man had disappeared, but he still sat on his heels beside her. He was looking up and talking to several more figures surrounding them. "I can't find any sign of fractures or internal bleeding. She probably has a concussion, but we'll have to chance moving her. It'll take more than an hour for the ambulance to get here from Valentine, and she's in shock. We can't leave her on the ground in the cold wind any longer."

This time when she tried to move her hand it responded, and she touched him on the thigh, which was the only part of him she could reach without moving. His leg was covered with a coarse fabric and felt hard as granite.

He looked down and put his hand over hers. "Hi again," he said softly. "I don't want to startle you, but I'm going to pick you up now and carry you to a car. The ambulance at Raindance is out of service, so we're going to drive you to the hospital. I'll try not to hurt you, but don't hesitate to holler if I do. Okay?"

She opened her mouth, but it felt funny—puffy and swollen—and she could taste blood. "Yes." The word came out with a lisp.

The man carefully worked one arm under her back and the other under her knees and lifted her. He rose effortlessly while holding her in his arms, and she clasped him around the neck, cradling her aching head in the hollow of his shoulder.

He walked over to a car and slid into the back seat. He didn't put her down, but held her on his lap while another man got behind the wheel and started the motor.

"Are you all right?" he asked against her ear. His breath was fresh and clean, and it tickled her cheek.

Again her "yes" was pronounced with a lisp, and it hurt to speak.

The man in front said something and the one holding her answered, but the voices seemed to come from far away. They continued to speak, but she was aware only of the strong arms holding her against the broad chest and the loud thumping of the heart beneath her ear. She felt safe even as she slipped once more into the painless void.

The scream of brakes and a sharp lurching motion tore through the fog of her consciousness, and she cried out and tightened her hold on the man's neck. "Dammit, Ox, take it easy," he thundered. "The poor kid's had enough bouncing around tonight."

"Ox?" She spoke the word even before it formed in her mind.

There were lights outside the car now, and she could see the man's mouth, so close to her own, turn up in a grin. "His name's Oxford, and he's the sheriff." He started to move forward on the seat. "I'm going to get out, so hang on and keep your head against my chest."

She buried her face against him as he maneuvered them both out of the car. A cold breeze hit her, and she moaned as it intensified the throbbing ache. The man sprinted through an open double glass door and into a building where once again it was warm. It was also light, and the brightness hurt her head. She closed her eyes and was lulled by the rhythm of his walk as he followed a voice down a corridor, then turned into a room.

"You can put her down here," the voice said, and she panicked.

"No," she cried and tightened her hold on him.

He continued to hold her. "It's okay, honey. I'll stay right here with you, but I've got to put you down so the doctor can examine you."

Honey. He'd called her honey, and it sounded warm and friendly, and infinitely comforting. She loosened her hold, and he laid her down gently on something high and narrow but thickly padded.

She grabbed for his hand before he could get away, and hung on. She was behaving like a child, but she couldn't help it. She needed someone to hold on to. Someone to care.

He folded her hand in one of his and stroked her cheek with the other. "Don't you want to open your eyes?"

"It hurts," she said, and he smoothed strands of hair back from her face.

They were joined then by another voice. "Rusty, what have you got here? What happened?"

So the man's name was Rusty.

"Hi, Vince. We had an accident just this side of Atwell. I'd turned out to pass, and she swerved and drove her car right into the truck. That clunker you call an ambulance is broken down again, so Ox and I brought her here in the patrol car. Couldn't leave her out there on the highway in the cold."

"So come to the next city council meeting and demand a new one. They don't want to take my word that we need it. Now, young lady, open your eyes and look at me."

Slowly she raised her lids and squinted at the man bending over her. He looked to be about forty and wore a white jacket over his striped dress shirt. His dark eyes were watching her. "What's your name?"

She opened her eyes a little wider. "I'm...I'm...M-my name is . . ."

Dear Lord, who was she? She couldn't remember her name!

She stiffened, and her fingernails dug into the top of the hand she was clinging to. "I don't know," she gasped. "I don't remember!"

"Don't be alarmed," said the man in the white coat. "You've had a head injury. It's not unusual to lose your memory for a while after something like that. It'll come back."

He started examining her in much the same way the first man had out on the highway. "Do you remember where you're from, or where you're going?"

She tried, but her mind was blank. "No," she moaned.

"That's all right," he said soothingly. "Just relax and don't try to force it. I'm Dr. Vincent Cole, and you're in the hospital in Raindance, Nebraska."

She recognized the name. "Raindance. That's where I was going."

The doctor smiled. "See. It's already coming back. Where's your purse? You probably have identification in it."

This time it was the other man who spoke. "Damn, I didn't even think of it. It's probably still in her car. Ox is having it towed to the garage in Atwell. I'll contact him and have him look for it."

He started to pull his hand away, but she clutched at it with both of hers. "No! Don't leave."

He stopped and let her hold on to him. "I won't if you don't want me to," he said reassuringly.

She felt like a fool. "I'm sorry," she whispered. "I— I'm so confused and afraid."

He leaned down and brushed his lips across her forehead. "Of course you are, but you don't need to be. I'll be right here with you."

She breathed a sigh of relief and felt a tear roll from the corner of her eye. What was happening to her? Who was she, and why was she on her way to Raindance, Nebraska?

She turned her head carefully and looked up at the man standing beside her. She hadn't been wrong about his size. He was tall, well over six feet, and she guessed his age at mid-thirties. Although he was apparently a truck driver, he dressed like a cowboy in faded jeans and a denim jacket with a plaid Western shirt and a dark Stetson hat. His features were rugged, but he had an open, friendly expression that lit up his face and was far more appealing than patrician bone structure.

The doctor spoke again. "You don't seem to have any broken bones, but we'll take some X rays to be sure. The nurse will help you out of your clothes so I can see if there's any other damage. Come on, Rusty, we'll step out in the hall."

"No!" The word was out before she could call it back, and she tightened her hold on him. "You promised you wouldn't leave. You promised."

She was in a state of panic, and although she recognized it, she couldn't control it. She didn't know who she was or why she was here, and she was totally alone and helpless except for this kind man. She knew she was being irrational, but she couldn't let him out of her sight. He might just walk away, and then she'd be left without anyone.

He glanced questioningly at the doctor, then looked down at her and again caressed her face with his big calloused hands. "That's right, honey, I promised, and Rusty Watt never goes back on his word. Ask the doc here. I just want to give you a little privacy while the nurse undresses you."

She was embarrassed to be behaving like such a baby, but she was terrified of being left alone without him. Taking a deep breath she managed to calm down a little. "All right," she said reluctantly, "but promise you'll come back?"

"Cross my heart," he said, and made an X across the left side of his chest.

She forced herself to release his other hand and watched him as he walked out the door with a jaunty, self-confident gait. She felt bereft.

"What's going on, Rusty?" Vince asked as they waited outside the examining room. "Do you know this girl? What happened?"

Rusty was asking himself the same questions. He shrugged. "Damned if I know, Vince. I never saw her before—until about an hour and a half ago when she rammed her car into my truck tractor. She can't be more than sixteen or seventeen, and she's scared to death.''

"Have you any idea where she's from?"

"Only that her car has Missouri license plates. It's odd. I drove behind her for several miles, and she drifted from one side of her lane to the other. She wasn't going very fast; that's why I decided to pass her. I'd pulled out and was driving beside her on the wrong side of the road when she crashed into me."

The doctor frowned. "Do you think she was drunk? I didn't smell liquor on her. She could have been high on drugs; I'll do blood tests."

"Is she going to be all right? The front of her car was caved in, and she was jammed against the steering wheel. She must have hit her head on it. Poor kid. It's a good thing she was wearing her seat belt. You will keep her in the hospital, won't you?"

"Yeah, but it looks like we're going to have to make room for you, too," he said with amusement. "She's not about to let you out of her sight. What in hell did you do to her?"

"Nothing." Rusty felt more than a little riled by the question. "She was unconscious when I got to her. I keep current on my advanced first-aid certificate—most truckers do—so I examined her and got her out of the car. I was afraid it might catch fire. I called Ox on the CB, and you know the rest."

Vince nodded. "When did she regain consciousness?"

Rusty rubbed the knotted muscles at the back of his neck and suddenly realized how exhausted he was. "Shortly after I got her out of the car. She sort of drifted in and out, but whenever I'd try to leave her she'd latch on to me and beg me to stay. Maybe I remind her of her father."

Vince snorted inelegantly. "Yeah, and I'm Florence Nightingale. We better get back in there before she starts tearing the place down looking for you. What are you going to do with her if she doesn't get her memory back right away?"

Rusty eyed him balefully. "What do you mean what am *I* going to do with her? I brought her to you."

Vince grinned. "Thanks, buddy, but I've got a wife who wouldn't understand. She doesn't let me bring home lost puppies, either."

Muttering an oath, Rusty headed back to the battered waif who'd been thrust so unexpectedly into his care. The nurse had dressed her in a green print hospital gown and covered her with a thin white blanket. When Rusty reached her side, she held up her hand like a child asking for protection, and he took it between both of his. It was small and took up hardly any room, he thought. So was she for that matter.

The blood and grime had been washed from her face, but the skin around her wide brown eyes was darkening, there was a narrow gash at her hairline, and her lower lip was swollen and cut. A small plastic bandage on her elegant little chin covered the deeper gash he knew was there.

Rusty saw the fear and confusion that clouded her eyes, and he felt a strong urge to reassure and protect her. Where were her parents? What was she doing traveling alone and apparently far from home? His eyes quickly swept the length of her and he wondered again how old she was.

"Thank you for coming back," she said carefully around her swollen lip.

"I told you I would." He fingered the long, thick blond braid that had been tossed forward onto her shoulder.

The doctor stood on the other side of the table and pulled the blanket down. Rusty divided his gaze between her face and the other side of the room while Vince examined her. Now and then she flinched or gasped, but she didn't cry out as the doctor probed. "You're going to be awfully stiff and sore for a while," he told her. "You're a mass of bruises, but nothing serious. We'll get those X rays now, and then put you in your room so you can sleep."

They wheeled her to another area and put a metal apron on Rusty so he could stand at the bottom of the table where she could see him while they took the pictures.

Although he waited calmly and patiently, his mind was going a mile a minute. How had he gotten himself into this? Just a few hours ago he'd been tooling down the highway listening to his favorite country and western music on the radio and looking forward to getting home and into his own bed. Now here he was in the hospital reassuring a terrified young woman that everything was going to be all right when it very well might not be.

He was tired. He'd driven all the way from the east coast pulling twin trailers before he'd delivered them in Omaha, and the last thing he wanted or needed was to play Daddy to some displaced teenager. He wanted to go home, have a couple of beers and sack out. Instead he was standing here smiling like an idiot and wondering if he was going to have to spend the night sitting up in a chair holding her hand.

Not that he objected to holding her hand. It was small and dainty, but she had one hell of a grip. He thought of the way she'd cuddled against him when he'd carried her in his arms. She'd been trembling with cold and shock and fear, and she'd held him tight and tucked her head into his shoulder with absolute trust. A shaft of anger startled him. Didn't she know how dangerous it was to snuggle up to a strange man like that? Hadn't her parents taught her anything?

An hour later she was settled in a room and had been given a mild painkiller that relaxed her and made her drowsy. The X rays had shown two cracked ribs, but the rest of her bone structure was intact. The concussion was painful but not dangerous, and Vince had told Rusty that she'd sleep through the night and he could go home.

Rusty bent over the bed and looked at the small, battered girl. She still clung to his hand, but now her grip was nominal as she slowly drifted into slumber. A wave of tenderness washed over him, and he leaned down to kiss her closed eyelids.

She stirred slightly. "Daddy?" she murmured past her split lip. "Oh, Daddy, I knew you weren't gone forever."

She smiled and returned to her dream.

Rusty gently pulled his hand from hers and settled the sheet and blanket around her shoulders. As he walked down the hall he saw Vince standing at the nurses' station and stopped beside him. "She's asleep. Are you sure she'll be all right if I leave?"

The doctor nodded. "She'll be fine, Romeo, but just in case, you will be home the rest of the night, won't you?"

Rusty grinned. "Where else? Oh, yes—just now when I kissed her good-night she called me 'Daddy.'"

He started to walk away, then turned and saluted. "Good night, Florence."

He turned again and sprinted toward the door as Vince muttered an unlaundered oath.

Chapter Two

The following morning Annelise woke with a throbbing ache from the top of her head all the way down to the soles of her feet. She'd decided not to attempt to open her eyes when she felt a big hand on her shoulder, and a deep voice said, "Come on, honey, wake up. It's breakfast time."

The first thing she saw as she tentatively cracked her eyelids open was a magnificent giant of a man standing beside the bed. Rusty! Her truck-driving guardian angel. He must have stayed with her even while she slept.

Instinctively she held up her hand, and he took it. She tried to smile but moaned when her dry lips cracked. He smiled instead, although there was sympathy in his hazel eyes. "Don't try to move around. I only came to let you know I'm here. The nurse will make you more comfortable, and I'll be back with your breakfast tray as soon as she's finished."

He squeezed her hand and left.

Half an hour later she'd been given a bed bath, had her mouth rinsed, and had her lips and face moisturized with a medicated cream. The nurse had unbraided her waist-length blond hair and brushed it as best she could under the circumstances. Annelise couldn't raise her head—it felt too much like bombs going off inside when she tried.

The nurse left, and moments later Rusty returned with a tray, which he put on the over-the-bed table. "Sorry about this," he said, as he eyed her breakfast with distaste. "All they've given you is chicken broth and custard. The coffee's for me, but you can have some if you want it."

She started to shake her head, then wished she hadn't as firecrackers exploded inside. He picked up the cup of broth and added a bent straw, then held it so she could sip. "Let's get some food in you. The nurse said when you've eaten everything she'll give you some more pain medicine."

He didn't seem to expect her to talk, but kept up a one-sided conversation while he fed her. When she'd finished eating and the nurse had given her a pill, he settled down in the chair beside the bed with his carafe of coffee.

Today he was again dressed in jeans and a Western-style shirt, and she noticed he was wearing pointed-toe boots. He also carried a cowboy hat, which he'd placed on top of the dresser, and she saw that his thick hair was dark brown with deep red highlights. "Have you been here all the time?" she asked.

"No. Once you fell asleep Vince said you'd be out for the night, so I went home. I came back early, though.

Didn't want you to be panic-stricken when you woke up.''

"I'm sorry I've been such a nuisance.'' She paused, embarrassed. "You're a very nice man.''

He winked. "Only to pretty little girls and frail old ladies.''

This time she did manage a smile. "But I don't fit in either category.''

He was immediately serious. "Do you know how old you are?''

"Of course. I'm twenty-two.''

He frowned. "I doubt that. What's your name?''

"Annelise Kelsey. Didn't I tell you this last night?''

"You said you couldn't remember.''

The sound of footsteps on the uncarpeted floor interrupted them, and Dr. Cole entered the room. He looked from Annelise to Rusty. "Still playing Daddy?'' he asked brightly.

"She says she's twenty-two years old,'' Rusty announced, outrage in every syllable. "I don't claim to be a saint, but damned if I'm going to be a father-figure to a grown woman.'' He looked at Annelise and grinned. "Would you settle for uncle?''

The doctor looked pleased. "Do you remember everything now?''

"Mostly,'' Annelise said. "I'm a little confused about the accident and what happened afterward, but my name is Annelise Kelsey, and I'm from Kansas City, Missouri. I'm going to be the new librarian here in Raindance.''

The doctor pulled up another chair and sat down. "That's great. Welcome to our town. Oh, by the way, the sheriff has your purse and will bring it to you sometime this morning. He wants to talk to you, too, but we'll put that off until you're feeling better. I need some information, though. Would you rather we talked alone?'' He glanced pointedly at Rusty.

The familiar stirrings of panic again assailed her. For heaven's sake, what was the matter with her? She'd never been like this before. She'd taken care of herself almost ever since she could remember, and this past summer she'd taken on the responsibility of her mother, too. She didn't need a man in her life, didn't even want one, so why was she so afraid to let this one out of her sight?

That concussion must have really scrambled her brain.

''I'd like Rusty to stay if he doesn't mind,'' she said, and looked at him apologetically. ''By the way, what's your last name?''

He took a swallow of the hot black coffee. ''Watt. Russell William Watt. I'm thirty-six years old and a truck jockey.''

''Truck jockey?''

''I drive a truck for a living.''

Dr. Cole lifted the clipboard he'd brought in and reached into his white jacket pocket for a pen. ''Annelise, I need a medical history on you.''

She answered all his questions, and when they were finished he sighed. ''I'd say you're one of the healthiest young women it's been my pleasure to interview. So what happened last night? Rusty says your car was weaving, and when he tried to pass, you drove right into him.''

Annelise was getting tired, and the accident was still hazy in her mind. She told him about not feeling well during the midafternoon, but when he asked her to describe her symptoms there really weren't any. Mostly just an inability to stay awake.

"And you didn't snap out of it even after you opened the window?" he asked.

"Only for a few minutes, then I had a strong attack of dizziness, and the next thing I remember is waking up on the ground with Rusty bending over me."

Vince frowned and continued to make notations on the official-looking form attached to the clipboard. "Has this ever happened before?"

"No, never."

"Do you often suffer from headaches, dizziness or nausea?"

"No. I recently had the complete physical that was required by the library board when I was hired, and I got a clean bill of health."

The doctor put the clipboard and pencil aside and cleared his throat. "In a city hospital the resident psychiatrist would take over the questioning now. But we're a small establishment and there are only two doctors—both family practitioners—in the area, so you're stuck with me. Would you object to answering some personal, nonmedical questions? I assure you, they're vital if we're to get a complete history."

Annelise hesitated. But he was a physician; why should she object to a few more questions? "I'll tell you anything I can," she said.

He glanced at the other man. "Maybe now you'd prefer that Rusty wait in the hall?"

For some reason she trusted Rusty more than she trusted the doctor, and besides, she didn't have anything to hide. "Why don't we wait and see what questions you're going to ask. Is that okay with you, Rusty?"

He nodded agreement. "Whatever you want."

Dr. Cole settled back in the chair and spoke in a friendly tone. "Have you had any personal problems lately? A broken romance? Pressure at college? Problems at work?"

Annelise closed her eyes and swallowed the lump of sadness that threatened to keep her from answering. "My father died in June, two weeks after I graduated from the university." Her voice was little more than a whisper.

Rusty reached over and took her hand, and she curled her fingers around his.

"I'm sorry," Vince said. "Did you have a close, loving relationship?"

She didn't want to talk about her dad. It opened up too many pits of anguish. "Not really," she said tightly. "He—he was gone a lot."

"Oh? Did he travel in his line of work? What was it?"

Annelise squirmed and wished she hadn't agreed so readily to this. "Yes, he was a salesman."

She told herself it wasn't actually a lie; he had been a salesman.

Vince nodded. "So he was on the road a good deal of the time?"

She hesitated. Oh, what difference did it make now? He was dead, and she wasn't going to weave fantasies around him anymore. "No, he hadn't been on the road for years. He was an alcoholic, and he died of cirrhosis of the liver," she said, her voice flat.

Rusty squeezed her hand, and she tightened her hold on his.

The doctor looked at her. "That would have been a difficult thing to live with." He was stating a truth, not offering sympathy.

"You might say that." She hated the bitterness she couldn't keep out of her voice. "It's not much fun to be the daughter of the neighborhood drunk, the object of pity and charity. Even with Mother working two jobs, we still fell below the poverty level. And Dad drank up part of what we did have."

She was tense and dry-eyed, and her head throbbed.

"You must have hated him," Vince said.

"I adored him. He was a miserable boozer who made my pretty mother an old woman before her time, but I loved him so much." Her voice caught on a sob, but she held it back.

Her free hand was clenched, and the other would have crushed Rusty's if his hadn't been so big and strong.

"If you loved him he must have had some admirable qualities," Vince said quietly.

Rusty spoke. "Vince, dammit all, can't you see..."

His words trailed off when he caught the warning glance the doctor threw at him.

"He had a lot of admirable qualities," Annelise said, without acknowledging the interruption. Her eyes burned with unshed tears, but she was determined not to let them fall. "He was kind and loving, and he used to make up bedtime stories to tell me. He was a good salesman, too—outgoing and friendly—and his company kept him on long after they'd have fired anyone else. But he had one weakness. He couldn't stop drinking. It ruined our lives and finally killed him.

"Did you cry when he died?"

Rusty looked like he was going to interrupt again, but he said nothing.

Annelise thought back. "No. I'd cried all the tears I had for him long before that. A-after he died I had to be s-s-strong for my mother."

"You don't have to be strong now," Vince said, and this time his tone was heavy with compassion. "Rusty has broad shoulders." He looked at the other man with a plea for understanding. "If you want to cry on one of them I'm sure he won't mind a bit."

That did it. A deep sob shook her, and the tears streamed down her face as Rusty bolted out of the chair and leaned over the bed to take her in his arms.

He pulled the sheet loose and wrapped her in it, then picked her up gently and sat back in the chair with her cradled on his lap. The anguish in her soul was greater than the throbbing pain from being moved around, and Annelise curled her arms around his neck, buried her face in his shoulder and wept. With a nod to Rusty, Vince left the room.

For a long time Rusty held her while she sobbed for the father she'd loved and hated with equal fervor. The lovable man who got sweeter and more gentle with every drink. Everyone liked him, drunk or sober, and even the employers who fired him did so with heavy hearts.

He'd been like a child, eager to please but not yet grown up enough to control his own destiny. He'd broken her mother's heart and health—but she'd forsaken family and security to stay with him. When he died, she'd died a little, too.

Annelise had finally calmed down when the nurse came in with a pill in a tiny plastic cup. She raised her eyebrows when she saw her patient curled up on Rusty's lap. "Does Dr. Cole know what's going on here?" Her tone was droll.

Annelise turned her embarrassed face into his chest as he chuckled. "Doc was the one who suggested it. Not that I wouldn't have thought of it eventually, you understand."

The nurse made a face. "I have every confidence in you, Rusty Watt. Now do you suppose you can loosen your hold on her for a second so she can take this pain pill? Then she's to sleep. Doctor's orders."

Annelise turned and took the pill and the glass of water the nurse handed her. When she'd swallowed it and handed back the glass, the nurse started to leave. "I mean it, Rusty. Put her to bed so she can rest. I'll be back in ten minutes to make sure you do."

"Yes ma'am, warden," he muttered good-naturedly as she swished out of the room.

He settled Annelise's head back on his shoulder and brushed a long strand of golden hair off her face. "Are you sure you're twenty-two?"

"Positive," she answered into his shirt.

"You don't look it. I thought you were sixteen."

"I'm not surprised. I've certainly been acting like a child. I'm sorry I've taken up so much of your time. You won't believe this, but I'm normally a very independent woman. I've worked since I was old enough to babysit, and I put myself through college. When my father died, my mother had an emotional breakdown, and I've been taking care of her all summer and fall."

His eyes were soft with compassion. "Then it's about time somebody took care of you for a while. I'm sorry we met the way we did, but I'm proud to be the one you trusted to keep you safe."

A sense of peace and well-being swept through her, and she smiled. "If the only way I could meet you was to run into you with my car, then I'm almost glad it happened. I'll be all right now, though. You don't have to bother with me anymore."

He touched her cheek with his lips. "Have you heard me complaining?"

"No, but—"

"Well, wait until you do before you apologize, okay?"

He lifted her and stood, then lowered her carefully onto the bed and covered her with the blanket. "I'm going to leave now and let you sleep, but I'll be back this evening."

The bed felt so good, and his voice had a lulling effect. "I'll look forward to it," she breathed, and was asleep before he got out the door.

Annelise slept until lunch, and again afterward, so she was feeling much better except for being shocked at the way she looked. She discovered the fold-down mirror on the over-the-bed table and looked with dismay at the face that stared back at her. There was an uneven cut high on her forehead, the skin around her eyes was dark and puffy, her lower lip was swollen and split, and there was a bandage on her chin.

She must have cried out at the sight, because the nurse came running in and took the mirror away from her. "I'm disfigured for life!" she cried, but the nurse, a different one with the change of shift, just smiled and shook her head.

"A week at the most," she said, "and you'll be pretty as ever. You're young and healthy. The cuts will heal without scars, and the discoloration around your eyes will fade fast." She stood back and cocked her head as her gaze roamed over Annelise's face. "Meanwhile, I could bring you a sack to put over your head...."

She broke into a teasing chuckle, and Annelise, unable to resist, joined her, then doubled over with her arms across her ribs. "Oh, please don't make me laugh," she gasped. "It hurts."

The nurse hurried to help her, but Annelise straightened gingerly. "I'm okay—it's just my battered muscles." She smiled. "Thanks for your offer, but I'd prefer a thick layer of makeup base. Did the sheriff ever bring my suitcases and purse?"

The nurse assured her that he had and that they'd been put away in her closet. Between them they covered most of the bruising around Annelise's eyes and brushed her long hair until it shone. She wanted to change into one of her own nightgowns, but she was still too sore to move around that much, so she settled for a fresh hospital gown.

Shortly after the supper trays were removed that evening, her headache had been tamed to a dull throb and she was sitting propped up in bed when Rusty and the doctor came in. "Hey, you're looking better," Rusty said as he took her hand.

"I feel better, thank you. Please sit down, both of you."

The men moved chairs to the side of the bed. "I see by your chart that you've slept most of the day and have a good appetite. Are you still in much pain?" the doctor asked.

"I'm pretty stiff and sore, but the headache's better."

"Good. You'll have to be careful of the ribs for a while, but we won't keep you here much longer. Where will you be living?"

The question startled Annelise. It was something she hadn't thought of since the accident. "Well, I—I don't know. I was planning to register at a motel when I got here and then look for an apartment."

"You can't go to a motel," Rusty thundered. "You'll need someone to look after you."

Annelise didn't much like the idea of being all alone when she was feeling so rocky, either, but she couldn't let him know that. She'd imposed on Rusty Watt far too much already.

She tried for a confident smile. "I'll be all right, really. I told you, I'm not normally such a crybaby."

Rusty opened his mouth to argue, but the doctor spoke first. "Rusty's right, a motel's no place for you to convalesce. We can keep you here through tomorrow, but after that your insurance company's going to get surly. Don't you know anybody in town?"

Her forced smile faded. "Not really. I've been corresponding with Mrs. Garrett, who's chairman of the library board, but I've never met her."

"Carol or Gwen Garrett?" Rusty asked.

"Carol. Do you know her?"

"Sure, her husband's my attorney. Gwen's her mother-in-law. Carol's a sweetheart—she'll find someplace for you to stay. If it's okay, I'll call her and ask her to come over tomorrow and talk to you."

Annelise nodded. "I guess you'd better. She said something in one of her letters about keeping an eye out for a vacant apartment, but she hasn't mentioned it since. The library's closed Sundays and Mondays, but

I'm due to start work on Tuesday. That's only five days away. I can't meet the public looking like this."

"With the skillful use of makeup you'll be presentable by then," the doctor said, "but meanwhile I don't want you to do anything but rest, get plenty of sleep and try to come to terms with your feelings about your father and his death."

Annelise's eyes widened with surprise. "I beg your pardon?"

Dr. Cole's gaze held hers. "I've been over your medical history thoroughly, and I even talked to your doctor in Kansas City. He in turn consulted with a psychiatrist, and the three of us agree that since there's nothing physically wrong with you, your sudden drowsiness and disorientation yesterday was probably a delayed grief syndrome."

"That's not true," she said, adamant in her denial. "I did grieve for my father. I've grieved for him all summer."

"You felt grief, but you didn't grieve," he said patiently. "You held it all in—you told me as much. You didn't cry or take advantage of any of the outlets of mourning. Instead you bottled it up, afraid to let it out because it would upset your mother even more than she already was."

Annelise frowned. "Well, yes, but—"

"Meanwhile," the doctor continued, "you felt guilty about your mixed love and hate feelings for him. You loved him as a father but you hated him as an abusive husband to your mother."

"He was never abusive!" Annelise sat straight up, and her eyes flashed fire. "He never touched my mother with anything but tenderness!"

Rusty said something to the doctor in an angry tone and started to stand but was quelled with a warning look and sank back down again.

"I'm sure he didn't," Dr. Cole said, "and I'm sorry. I should have chosen a better word. The term 'abuse' has several connotations. I didn't mean to imply that he was physically violent, but I'm sure there were many times when you were growing up that he made promises he didn't keep, was very late getting home and then arrived drunk, and embarrassed both you and your mother in front of friends."

Annelise sank back against the pillows and closed her eyes. "Yes, those things were commonplace."

"And you were furious with him because he was so unreliable and caused you and your mother so much worry." It was a statement, not a question.

"Yes." Just talking about it brought back the turmoil of emotions: anger, fear, shame and, not least, love.

"You're not alone, you know." The doctor's tone was kind and soothing. "All families of alcoholics have these feelings. Did you and your mother ever contact Al-Anon?"

She opened her eyes. "No. For a long time we didn't know about it, and once we did we were too busy and tired and ashamed to go. I realize now that was a mistake, but..."

Dr. Cole leaned forward and patted her hand, then stood. "It's all over, and the best thing you can do for yourself and your mother is put it behind you. Now that you've had a good cry and talked about your feelings, you're going to be fine. Remember your father with love and work at forgiving him for his weaknesses."

She felt the soft tickle of a tear as it rolled down her cheek. "I will. Thank you."

He left then, and Rusty followed a few minutes later after promising to see her the next day.

When Rusty arrived the following morning he was accompanied by a stunningly beautiful raven-haired woman with deep blue eyes and a happy, contented look. She was also quite obviously pregnant.

He introduced her as Carol Garrett, and Carol smiled. "I'm so sorry about your accident. Everyone in town has heard about it. In a community of less than twenty-five hundred people there are few secrets, but we had no idea our new librarian was the one involved. Are you going to be all right?"

Annelise was sitting up in bed, and her aches and pains had eased considerably. "Oh, yes. I'll be dismissed from the hospital tomorrow, but I'm not sure how long it will be before I look human again and can get around without difficulty."

"That's what I wanted to talk to you about," Carol said. "Rusty says you need a place to go when you leave here, and my husband and I would like you to stay with us until you find an apartment."

Annelise was cheered by the other woman's friendly generosity, but she didn't want to be a burden. "That's awfully nice of you, but it's not necessary. I can go to a motel."

Carol shook her head. "We wouldn't hear of it. You shouldn't be alone in a strange town while you're still recuperating. Bryce and I have plenty of room. We've recently moved into our new home, and it has two spare bedrooms as well as a nursery." She patted her swelling abdomen absently.

Annelise could feel the excitement that radiated from Carol. "When's the baby due?"

"December," she said happily. "Not a very nice thing to do to the poor child, giving him a birthday right at Christmas time, but we'll make sure it's always special."

Annelise laughed. "Do you know it's a boy, or is it wishful thinking?"

Carol joined in the laughter. "Actually, neither. We didn't want to call the baby 'it' so Bryce started using the masculine gender. He claims it has nothing to do with preference, but I know he'd like a son."

"Do you have other children?"

"No, this is our first, but we'd like several more. That's the reason for all the bedrooms, although it'll take us a while to fill them."

Rusty glanced at his watch and interrupted. "Look, ladies, could you get back to the matter at hand and chat later? I have to go to Atwell and see the mechanic about Annelise's car and my truck tractor, and I'd like to get the problem of where she's going to be staying settled first. I'll need an address and phone number to give them at the garage."

Annelise felt a stab of guilt. "Oh, Rusty, I'm sorry. I've never even asked about your truck. Was it badly damaged? I have insurance, of course."

"You've had enough to worry about," he said softly. "The damage to the tractor was minimal—a few dents and scratches that will need some body work. Your little Plymouth's the one that took all the punishment. It may not be worth fixing."

"Oh, no!" She should have known the car would be a wreck. It was too lightweight to survive a collision with a truck.

"Now don't you worry about it," Rusty admonished. "We'll get it taken care of, but the mechanic will want to talk to you. Shall I give him the Garretts' phone number?"

"Yes, of course," Carol answered for her. "There's a bedroom on the ground floor that will be just right for her. She won't have to climb stairs." She leaned over and put her hand on Annelise's. "You will come, won't you? I have a couple of leads on apartments, so it shouldn't be for long."

Annelise felt an almost overwhelming sense of relief. She'd dreaded the thought of going to an impersonal and lonely motel room. "Thank you," she said thickly. "I'd love to, if you're sure it won't be putting you out."

They agreed that Rusty would pick her up at the hospital early the next afternoon and drive her to the Garretts', then Rusty and Carol said goodbye and left.

Annelise was dressed in brown slacks and a matching sweater with a turquoise Indian design that snugly outlined the ample curve of her breasts as she waited for Rusty on Saturday.

It was too uncomfortable for her to put her arms up to braid her long hair, so the nurse had tied it back with a brown print scarf at her nape instead. Although her face was still somewhat discolored, the swelling was gone, the cuts were healing, and a liberal application of makeup camouflaged the worst of it.

Her muscles were still stiff and her ribs were sore, so she moved around slowly and with care, but there was no dizziness or nausea. In spite of the discomfort it was great to be out of bed and walking around. She'd never again take her mobility for granted.

When Rusty arrived shortly after lunch, Annelise was standing at the window looking out across the barren grounds. The few trees were naked of leaves and swayed in the wind that howled at the cloud-laden sky and blew bits of paper and sticks ahead of it.

"What are you doing out of bed and with your clothes on?" a familiar voice behind her asked.

She turned and smiled at Rusty as he came toward her. Today he was wearing the Stetson hat he usually carried when he was indoors. "It's generally considered good form to dress before going out in public," she said primly, but she felt her lips turn up in a mischievous smile.

"Your form's good enough just the way it is," he answered, and made a production of looking her over from chin to ankles. "Whatever became of my little teenager? You've got the curves of a woman." His tone was teasingly outraged.

"That happens to teenagers when they grow up to be twenty-two," she informed him with a jaunty grin.

"Not usually as well as it's happened to you, honey." This time the amusement was gone, and he was serious. "I can see I'm going to have to behave more like a gentleman and less like an affectionate uncle. Are you ready to leave?"

"Yes, the doctor's already signed me out. What did you find out about my car yesterday? Are they going to be able to fix it?"

He shook his head. "The mechanic advises against even trying. My truck's covered by your insurance, but I doubt that you'll get anything."

Her heart sank. She couldn't afford to buy another car. She barely had enough money to tide her over un-

til she got settled and started receiving regular pay-
checks.

Just then the nurse came pushing a wheelchair. "I
saw you come in, Rusty," she said cheerfully, "so I
figured I'd better get here before you start carrying my
patient around again."

His eyes widened with mock indignation. "You mean
I don't get to cuddle her up anymore? Hell, Sue Ellen,
what kind of hospital you runnin' here?"

The nurse winked at him. "The most professional
kind. You'll have to wait till we get her out the door for
that."

"You're a hard woman. Just wait and see if I bring
you any more of my business," he muttered as he
helped Annelise into the chair.

Outside he helped her into his aging blue Ford
Bronco, then went around and got in on the other side.
"You haven't seen our town yet," he said as he drove
out of the parking lot. "Would you like the grand tour
on our way to the Garretts'?"

Annelise settled comfortably into the upholstered
seat. "I'd like that if you have the time."

Raindance was built on either side of Highway 20 in
northwestern Nebraska, with mostly commerce to the
south and predominantly residences to the north. The
hospital was in the southeastern section, several blocks
from Main Street, the town's four-block business district that began at the highway and ended at the rail-
road tracks. Rusty pointed out the school grounds, the
funeral parlor, the movie theater and, once they turned
onto Main Street, the various shops, markets and of-
fices that lined the wide paved road. The library was a
fairly new brick building on the north side, in one corner of the large city park that also housed the court-

house. Rusty explained with pride that Raindance was the county seat.

Annelise had to restrain herself from asking him to stop so she could go in the library and see where she was to start her career, but she knew the Garretts were waiting. Anyway, Rusty no doubt had better ways to spend the afternoon than acting as tour guide to her.

The Garretts' home was on the northern outskirts of town near the golf course. It was a large house, obviously new, set amid huge old pine, oak and elm trees on at least an acre of land. Rusty drove up the long graveled driveway and stopped at the side of the house.

Before he could lift Annelise down, Carol appeared on the porch accompanied by a tall, handsome man with dark blond hair and brown eyes.

Rusty put his arm around Annelise's waist as he helped her walk over the rough terrain to the house. "Hi," Carol called, as they started up the steps. "How are you feeling?"

Annelise smiled at her hostess. "Much better, thank you. I'm still a little stiff, but that will work itself out."

Carol introduced the man beside her as her husband, Bryce Garrett. He took Annelise's hand. "Welcome. Sorry you've been injured, but we're pleased that you'll be staying with us for a while." He turned to Rusty and punched him on the arm. "Hi, pal, I won't ask what you've been up to. You're the only guy I know who can be involved in an auto accident and come out of it without a scratch. Come on, I'll help you with the suitcases and then we'll have a beer."

The inside of the house was both luxurious and homey. The large rooms were light and airy, and the furniture was new and expensive. It was exactly the type of home Annelise had always dreamed of someday living in. She shuddered as she thought of the tiny, dark, sparsely furnished house in the rough, run-down neighborhood where her family had spent the past ten years.

Annelise was shown to a bedroom across the hall from the bathroom. It was furnished in cherry-wood, with carpeting in deep rose and a bedspread and curtains in a lighter shade of the same color.

"Oh, it's so beautiful," she breathed.

Carol put her arm around Annelise's shoulders. "I hope you'll be comfortable. Do you feel up to visiting for a while, or would you rather go back to bed?"

Annelise was a little tired from the unaccustomed exertion, but she in no way wanted to get back in bed. "I'm fine, and I'd love to visit. I'll unpack later."

The four of them spent a comfortable hour in the living room. The Raindance natives took turns explaining to Annelise the character of the town that had recently celebrated its centennial. "We're sometimes a little slow to make changes," Bryce explained, "but a hefty percentage of our high-school seniors go on to college, our church attendance is well above average, and our hospital is ranked as one of the best small medical facilities in the state. Now that you're here, I'm sure our library will be upgraded, too."

"Is something wrong with the library?" she asked, puzzled by his statement.

"Not really," Carol assured her, "But Miss Dillingham had been there too long and was too old to do the job properly for the past few years. No one had the heart to forcibly retire her, but we finally persuaded her she should stop working and do some of the traveling she'd always talked about."

Carol chuckled. "The whole town turned out for her going-away dinner and gave her a set of luggage. She's now touring Europe with a senior citizens' group, and we have you."

In the pause that followed, Rusty put down his empty beer bottle and looked at his watch. "I've got to be on my way," he said, rising to his feet. "I'm driving the tractor to Omaha tomorrow for some body work, and then I've got a load to haul to Los Angeles. I'll be gone a week or so, and there are a lot of things to take care of before I leave."

Annelise squeezed her lips shut to hold back the protest that nearly escaped. It was none of her business if he was leaving town, but why did it have to be so soon? She'd assumed he'd be here.

Even as the thoughts entered her mind she knew they didn't make sense. Just because he'd taken care of her after the accident didn't mean he was responsible for her. Maybe Dr. Cole was right—she did seem to be looking for a father. It was just as well Rusty was leaving. He made it too easy for her to lean on him.

Bryce and Carol stood, too, and thanked Rusty for bringing Annelise to the house.

Annelise winced as her muscles protested the strain put on them when she struggled to rise from the upholstered chair. Rusty was immediately beside her, lifting her. "You shouldn't have tried to stand," he scolded gently, "but now that you're up you'd better go back to bed."

He took her arm and led her to the front door, then turned to look at Bryce and Carol. "Take good care of my foundling while I'm gone," he said as he shook hands with Bryce and kissed Carol on the cheek.

They assured him they would, then headed in the direction of the kitchen, leaving Rusty and Annelise alone. He put his arm around her waist, and his glance searched her face. "Will you be all right now? Promise to keep your appointment with the doctor on Monday afternoon, and don't start work on Tuesday unless you feel up to it."

It was no wonder she was so dependent on him. He made it difficult not to be.

She managed a passable smile. "I'll be fine, thank you. Be careful, Rusty. Stay out of the way of people like me who don't have sense enough to get off the road when they're not in any shape to drive."

Her voice broke, and she stopped talking.

He leaned down and she knew he intended to kiss her on the forehead, but without planning it or meaning to she raised her face and his lips touched hers and clung.

It was a sensation she'd never before experienced. A sense of coming to life; a heightened excitement that rippled through her body and made her aware of her sensuality in a way that bonded her to this man who could coax such a response from her. Rusty felt it, too. She could tell by the sudden clenching of his hand at her waist and the tension that raced through his hard muscles. She heard his quick intake of breath as he pulled her closer and his mouth moved restlessly over hers.

Long before she was ready he released her and sprinted toward the Bronco.

Chapter Three

Rusty clenched the steering wheel and tore down the two-lane gravel road that led back into Raindance as he mentally cursed himself. What was the matter with him that he'd react like that to a brotherly kiss with a young girl?

Well, she wasn't actually a girl. When he'd held her against him she was clearly all woman.... But she was only barely out of her teens and way too young for him, he reminded himself sternly. Still, that kiss was anything but brotherly, although that was all he'd intended. He hadn't even been aiming for her mouth, but it had somehow gotten in the way. And when his lips touched hers the jolt he'd gotten had been unexpected and as unwelcome as it was enticing. It had taken all his control not to crush her to him. He'd had to forcibly tear himself away, and he was still tingling at the thought.

He slowed the Bronco as he entered the residential streets. That little lady was lethal, and it was a good thing he was leaving town tomorrow. It'd probably take him the whole week to cool down.

Rusty sighed and relaxed his grip on the wheels. Well, never let it be said that Rusty Watt didn't learn from an experience once it kicked him in the . . . uh . . . teeth. No more devoted uncle routine with Miss Annelise Kelsey! Hereafter he'd stand on the other side of the room and keep his hands clasped behind his back when she was in the vicinity.

She was a sweet kid, but that was exactly the problem—she was a kid. He'd even bet almost anything that she was still a virgin. She had that air of innocence about her that screamed *untouched*.

He wiped a hand tiredly up over his forehead, tilting his hat back. Great. More power to her. He certainly wasn't going to be the one to deflower her. He'd leave that up to a boy her own age.

Rusty's stomach knotted suddenly, and he was appalled to realize that the thought of any other man making love to Annelise made him want to hit something.

Annelise leaned against the closed door and took a series of deep breaths. She throbbed in parts of her that she hadn't even known had nerves! None of the guys she'd dated had ever affected her that way before.

She'd only wanted to kiss Rusty goodbye. He'd been so kind and thoughtful, and he'd spent such a lot of time making sure she got good care at the hospital. He'd even seen to it that she had a place to go when she was released, and she'd wanted him to know how much she appreciated his concern.

Her hands moved up to her warm, flushed face. He knew now for sure. She'd reacted like a magnet when his mouth had touched hers. She'd been kissed before, but no one had lit this strange fire in her that Rusty had. What must he think of her? She'd even clung to him when he'd pulled away from her. How could she ever face him again?

When her heartbeat had slowed to normal and she was reasonably sure the flush had faded from her cheeks, she went into the kitchen, only to walk in on Carol and Bryce in a loving embrace. They turned as she entered and laughed when she stammered an apology and started to back out.

"Hey, it's legal, we're married," Carol teased as she moved out of Bryce's arms. "We have a license and everything."

Annelise quickly regained her composure. "Well, you certainly don't act like it," she said with a grin. "Who ever heard of a wife smooching in the kitchen with her own husband? You two must not have been married long".

"Two years."

"Twelve years."

They spoke at the same time, then chuckled at their conflicting answers. "We were married right after I graduated from high school," Carol explained, "but we had problems and were divorced two years later, and I moved away. Two years ago I came back to take care of some business for my mother, and we discovered we were still in love, so we were married again." She looked at her husband adoringly. "This time it's forever."

Annelise suspected there was a great deal more to the story, and hoped someday Carol would tell her all of it.

* * *

Annelise met most of the town's leading citizens and library patrons at a reception in her honor sponsored by the library board on Tuesday, her first day on the job. A huge, colorful banner, proclaiming Welcome Annelise Kelsey, was strung across the wall behind her desk, and coffee and cookies were served all day by the board as people flocked to introduce themselves and get a look at the pretty, new—and *young*—librarian who had come to town with such a bang.

Everyone knew about the accident, and Annelise found that instead of being interested in her educational qualifications, they wanted all the details of her hospital stay. Carol had warned her small-town living took some getting used to. Annelise was essentially a very private person. Her background of poverty and shame at her father's drunkenness had made her that way, and it was difficult for her to answer personal questions. She soon found, however, that the townspeople's interest was rooted in friendly curiosity rather than rude prying, and she learned to graciously turn away the questions she didn't want to answer and accept the friendliness at face value.

The mayor, James Farr, and his wife, Margaret, invited Annelise to their home for dinner the following Friday and told her their son, Lance, who was taking a semester off from his studies at Harvard University to work on his Ph.D. dissertation, would be joining them.

That evening when she mentioned the invitation to Bryce and Carol at the dinner table, Bryce gave her a brief sketch of the family. "The Farrs are pioneer stock," he said. "Jim's great-grandfather was one of the first settlers in Raindance. In fact the town was built on what was originally his ranch. Over the generations his family has made a lot of money on land and wise investments. His grandfather built the first lumberyard in the area and Jim still owns it, but his real love is politics. He's been mayor for ten years and is getting ready to run for the legislature next election."

Bryce grinned and added, "Sounds like he's trying to fix you up with his son. Lance is a good kid. About twenty-five and bright. Top of his class at Harvard, which I needn't tell you isn't easy. He's got the single-minded determination to get ahead far and fast. If you're looking for a husband, you couldn't do better."

"Bryce, for heaven's sake, don't start matchmaking," Carol protested. "Lance is about as exciting as a limp noodle. A rich limp noodle, but a limp noodle all the same."

Annelise smiled to lighten her tone. "I'm not in the market for a husband right now, but I'll file him away for future reference. Sounds like just what I'll be looking for."

Carol simulated a look of horror. "Surely you jest," she cried dramatically.

"Not at all." Annelise was no longer smiling. "I figure it's just as easy to fall in love with a rich man as a poor man."

Determinedly she pushed aside the lingering memory of the passion Rusty's kiss had stirred in her.

Carol's expression changed to real concern. "You don't mean that!"

"Yes I do." Her gaze sought Carol's. "You've said your dad was a banker before he retired. I imagine that means your family was comfortably well off?"

"Well, yes, but—"

"Mine wasn't." Annelise's tone was bleak. "My dad was...uh...sick, and my mother had no marketable skills. Mom worked when she could, but part of the time we were on welfare. It was awful, and it left scars that won't go away. I made up my mind a long time ago to get a good education so I could support myself, and I'm still working on that. However, I'd like to have children so I'll probably marry someday—but only to a man with money, lots of it. My children will never know the humiliation of accepting charity."

Carol opened her mouth to protest, but Bryce quickly changed the subject. "I think we're ready for dessert, honey. Isn't that apple pie I've been smelling?"

By Friday evening the bruises on Annelise's face were almost completely faded, and only a light film of make-up base was needed. She added blusher to her high cheekbones, a touch of green eye shadow to her eyelids and apricot gloss to her lips to hide the roughness from small scars not yet totally healed.

The dress she chose to wear to dinner with the mayor and his family was an avocado lightweight wool. She'd always made most of her clothes, and she bought designer patterns that were elegant when fashioned in good-quality materials.

Although at work she wore her long golden hair in either a topknot or a chignon, she preferred to leave it down or in a thick braid at other times. Tonight she tied it back at the nape with one of her numerous scarves, this one in a matching shade of avocado with a pattern in gold, orange and black.

Since she had no car she had to rely on others for transportation. She'd been riding to work with Bryce every morning at eight and acquainting herself with the joys and the problems of the library until she opened it to the public at ten o'clock. Not that she couldn't have walked. She'd done a lot of that during her growing-up years, but since the Garretts lived a couple of miles out of town in a new subdivision, Bryce insisted on driving her in.

On this evening Carol drove Annelise to the mayor's home, one of a number of big older houses not far from the city park. Margaret Farr, an attractive middle-aged woman whose white-streaked dark hair was arranged in a rather dated beauty-shop wave, greeted her warmly at the door and led her into the comfortable living room where the mayor clasped her hand and told her to call him Jim. "Only use James for political purposes," he said jovially, then turned to the younger man standing a few feet away. "This is our son, Lance, our new librarian, Miss Kelsey."

"Annelise," she corrected, and extended her hand.

Lance Farr was the same height as his father—about five-foot-nine—but unlike Jim, who was portly, Lance was slender to the point of being gaunt. His thin sandy-colored hair was already starting to recede at the temples, and he wore dark-framed glasses too large for his thin face. He was the type of colorless man who tended to blend into the woodwork until you looked past the glasses and into his alert, intelligent and probing gray eyes.

His shy smile added an extra dimension to his undistinguished features as he took her hand. "Welcome to Raindance, Annelise," he said in a voice that was strong and pleasant.

The meal was the standard meat-and-potatoes fare of the midwestern cattle country, and the Farrs were solid, down-to-earth people, although Jim tended to dominate the conversation and Lance spoke little. When the evening was over Lance offered to drive Annelise back to the Garretts'.

His car was a fairly new Chevrolet Celebrity, and when Annelise admired it he shrugged. "I wanted a Toyota, but Dad insists that we shop locally, and the only two car dealers in Raindance are Ford and Chevrolet."

She chuckled. "Don't expect sympathy from me. I'd settle for a bicycle. I hate having to rely on other people for transportation. I'd hoped to be in an apartment closer to the library by now."

Lance pulled up in front of the Garretts' house and shut off the engine. "That might not be easy," he said, settling more comfortably into the seat. "In a town this size the residents are older, more settled, and most of them own or rent homes. We only have one apartment building and it contains four units. There hasn't been a vacancy there in years, but some of the people who live in the big older houses have remodeled a few of their rooms into makeshift apartments. Then, too, there's Mrs. York's rooming house—but it's on the southern outskirts of town, and she's usually filled up."

Annelise sighed. "I'm finding that out. Carol took me to Trent Realty, and even they didn't have any leads. I can't impose on the Garretts much longer, but no way could I afford to stay in a motel."

Lance was silent for a moment. "Let me think about it. Maybe I can come up with something. Would you consider moving in with someone else?"

Annelise's head jerked up with surprise. Was this going to be a proposition? She hadn't expected that of him.

"It would depend on whether it was a man or a woman," she said tightly.

She couldn't see his expression in the dark, but his tone was repentant. "Oh, hey, I didn't mean ... I guess you couldn't be expected to know it, but men and women don't live together openly in Raindance. Not if they value their reputations, that is. These small rural towns still have old-fashioned moral standards."

Annelise felt silly. "I'm sorry, it's just that ... well, things are different in the city. Sure, I'd share a house or an apartment with another woman if we were compatible. I'd even consider a basement or an attic. I'm getting desperate."

Lance opened his door, got out and came around to help Annelise out of the car. It was cold, and she pulled her coat closer around her neck. The porch light was on, and Lance unlocked the door with her key but held it shut as he turned to her. "Would you like to go to the movies with me tomorrow night? They're showing a rerun of *Dr. Zhivago*. You've probably seen it, but it's well worth watching again."

"Yes, I have seen it, and I agree. I'd love to go with you," Annelise said with a warm smile.

Lance said good-night and left, but as Annelise got ready for bed it wasn't her coming date with him that occupied her mind. It was Rusty Watt. He'd left town on Sunday and said he'd be gone about a week. Tomorrow was Saturday, so he'd probably be back in town within the next couple of days.

She pulled her long-sleeved flannel nightgown over her head and crawled into bed. She'd missed him more than she wanted to admit. Every night she'd fallen asleep with the memory of his arms around her, his lips gently ravaging her own.

Annelise snuggled deeper under the covers. The feelings she'd experienced with Rusty were as disturbing as they were thrilling. She was in no hurry to marry, and even if she had been, Rusty wasn't in the running as a candidate for husband.

He was a truck driver, which ruled out his being rich. He probably had no more than a high-school education, which made it unlikely he'd ever be truly successful, and he dressed like a cowboy in jeans, boots and a Stetson hat. She doubted if he even owned a business suit. Annelise had worn too many thrift-shop discards when she was growing up—her sights were set on designer clothes, both for herself and for her husband.

She felt a twinge of self-disgust. If she put her thoughts into words she'd sound like the worst kind of snob, when she'd never had anything to be snobbish about.

Her father had been her only male role model, and, although she'd loved him, he'd let her down every time she'd needed him, she thought, trying to justify her feelings. Maybe that's why she clung so tenaciously to her ideal of the perfect husband. She wanted someone to be proud of, someone who would enhance her instead of embarrassing her, someone who would take care of her instead of needing to be taken care of.

Was it so awful to want a Prince Charming for a husband? Or was Prince Charming only a fictional character in a fairy tale? Would she break her own heart and turn herself into a selfish, grasping woman while looking for a man who didn't exist?

Annelise watched the front door of the library all day Saturday, hoping Rusty would walk through it. She knew she was being inconsistent, but she couldn't help looking up every time it opened.

He didn't walk through, though, and neither did he call that evening while she was out with Lance. She resisted the urge to ask Carol, but she knew the other woman would have told her if he had. Oh well, he'd probably get in tomorrow.

She'd enjoyed going to the movie with Lance, although the small size of the theater had been a shock— even the movie houses in the malls in Kansas City were bigger. But this one had been nearly filled with patrons.

Lance bought her hot buttered popcorn and, at intermission, a cola. When the show was over they stopped at The Ice Cream Shoppe on Main Street for banana splits and sat laughing at the antics of a gang of noisy teenagers partying with sodas and sundaes.

"I missed all of this when I was in high school," Annelise said, as she giggled at a silly joke one of them told. "I worked at a fast-food stand on weekends and babysat in the evenings."

Lance looked at her soberly. "I missed it, too. I was the class egghead. Not husky or coordinated enough for sports and not interested in the latest rock group. I spent most of my spare time studying or reading. As a result I was senior class valedictorian—and probably the only boy in school who was still a virgin."

Annelise could hear the heartache and loneliness in his tone, and she put her hand over his on the table. "The teen years aren't always all they're cracked up to be, are they?"

He turned his hand and squeezed hers. "No, but most of us manage to blunder through them and turn out to be reasonably happy adults. Are you happy now, Annelise?"

"Yes," she said slowly. "Sad or discontented at times, but underneath I'd say I'm happy. You?"

He nodded. "I enjoy learning, and I'm looking forward to completing my doctorate. Oh, and in case you're wondering," he smiled shyly and flushed "—I'm no longer a virgin."

She felt the color rising in her cheeks, also. "Congratulations. I'm afraid I am."

"Then you're the one to be congratulated," he said, still holding her hand. "Stay that way until you fall in love. Without that, the experience is highly overrated."

Annelise didn't hear from Rusty on Sunday, or Monday, or Tuesday, and when she finally broke down and asked Bryce if he was back yet, Bryce said he hadn't seen him.

Halloween was coming up on Saturday of that week, so on Wednesday morning Annelise used the hours from eight to ten to start decorating the library with pumpkins and witches and black cats made by the high-school art classes.

Since there was no money in the overextended budget for that sort of thing, Annelise had called the school the week before and asked if they'd be interested in supplying original designs made by the students. The art teacher had been delighted to have a project that would be put on public display, and the students had come up with some really innovative goblins.

At ten o'clock she unlocked the door to find two of her regular patrons waiting with books to return in their arms, impatient to check out some more. While they browsed Annelise got the tall ladder out of the storeroom, positioned it between two rows of shelves and climbed to the top with an oversize flying cardboard witch in one hand and a box of thumbtacks in the other.

Letting go of the ladder, she stretched to tack the yarn supporting the witch to the rafter. Still unable to reach, she was stretching further when a pair of large hands clamped around her hips and a voice sharp with irritation said softly, "You never learn, do you? First I have to pull you out of a wrecked car, and now, if I'd been a few seconds later, I'd have had to scoop you up off the floor."

"Rusty!" She turned so fast that she lost her balance and literally fell into his arms.

The big man hugged her, and she hugged him back, thankful for the privacy provided between the two tall bookcases. He was holding her with her feet off the floor, and his cheek when it pressed against hers was cold. His sheepskin-lined denim jacket was bulky between them, and a cowboy hat covered his mahogany-colored hair.

"I ought to give you a proper scolding," he growled. "You need a keeper."

"I was perfectly safe until you came along and startled me," she protested. "Did you just get in?"

He hesitated. "No, I got home Monday afternoon."

Suddenly all the joy went out of her, and she involuntarily stiffened in his embrace. So much for her stupid notion that he might miss her as she'd missed him. He'd been back two days before he'd bothered to come and say hello.

Numb with disappointment Annelise unwound her arms from around his neck and pushed against his shoulders. "Put me down," she ordered, and was dismayed to hear the hurt in her tone.

He let her slide slowly until her feet touched the floor, but he kept one arm around her waist as he tilted her chin up with his other hand.

She saw that the happy expression was gone from his features, too, as he scrutinized her face. "I knew you'd be beautiful when the bruises healed," he said huskily, "and I wasn't wrong. How are your ribs? Was I too rough when I hugged you?" His hand gently brushed her rib cage.

His concern for her was genuine and touching, but she realized now that it was only that. Concern for a young woman who had been injured in an accident in which he was also involved. Apparently he hadn't been at all affected by that kiss that had nearly devastated her. She was glad she hadn't had a chance to make a complete fool of herself before she found out.

"I'm fine, thank you." She was determined to keep the conversation friendly but impersonal. "Most of my bruises are gone, and the ribs are healing nicely."

She backed away from him. "Now, if you'll excuse me I have to finish putting up the decorations." She was relieved to note that her tone was sufficiently business-like.

"Oh, no you don't," he said, and started up the ladder. "I'll do it. Hand me that witch and another tack."

Rusty's tone showed he would brook no argument, and Annelise picked up the cardboard figure from the floor and handed it to him along with the box of tacks.

They worked together for half an hour, and when they were finished the library had taken on a festive air. Rusty stood back and surveyed their handiwork. "You say the high-school kids created all this? There's a lot of talent in that class."

"Yes there is," Annelise agreed, and started to lift the ladder.

"I'll do that," Rusty said, taking it from her. "Just show me where it goes."

She led the way to the storeroom and pointed out the space where it had stood. After waiting so long for him to get back to town, she wished now that he'd leave. It was difficult for her not to stare at him with her heart in her eyes. He was so darned *male*. Every time he stretched or climbed up and down the ladder, the muscles in his denim-encased thighs, legs and buttocks rippled.

Again she just managed to tear her gaze away from him before he turned around and caught her ogling. "Well, that's done," he said, dusting the palms of his hands against his jeans. "Do I have your solemn word you won't go near that ladder again? Last I knew there was a big hulking custodian around here who can reach the high places for you."

She wrinkled her nose. "I don't need a man. I'm perfectly capable of doing things for myself, thank you."

"And that includes breaking your pretty neck," he muttered. "How about having dinner with me tonight?"

Annelise blinked, confused by his abrupt change of topic. "I—I'm sure you have better things to do than take me to dinner."

She knew she sounded rude, but she had to turn him down quickly before she gave in to the urge to say yes. She didn't want him to take her out because of some misplaced sense of responsibility.

"If I did I wouldn't have asked you, now would I? I'll pick you up at the Garretts' at six-thirty."

"How do you know I'm still living with Bryce and Carol?" she challenged.

Rusty grinned and put his finger on the tip of her nose. "Honey, haven't you learned yet that everybody knows everybody else's business in a small town? Be ready when I get there, I'm going to be hungry."

The wicked gleam in his eye as he turned and walked away left Annelise wondering just what he was going to be hungry for.

Annelise was dressed in gray wool slacks and a pink sweater when Rusty arrived at the Garretts' to pick her up that evening. He was wearing Western pants and a soft leather jacket with his ever-present Stetson and boots.

Bryce offered Rusty a beer, and Annelise and Carol each had a soft drink. Annelise didn't drink, but if she did it wouldn't have been beer. She was the white wine and champagne type, she decided. She'd never been impressed with men who drank beer either. She wished Rusty wasn't so fond of it. One more reason why she mustn't let her feelings for him get out of hand, she told herself firmly.

That was going to be difficult, though, when her pulse raced and her temperature rose every time he came near her.

They went to a restaurant called the Steak and Stein at the eastern outskirts of town on the highway. It was situated next to the Raindance Inn, the fanciest of the area's two motels, and drew diners from town as well as guests from the inn and tourists driving through on the highway.

Tonight the parking lot was nearly full, and they got the last table in the restaurant, a curved booth with a thickly padded maroon vinyl seat. The brassy blond waitress greeted them enthusiastically. "Hi, Rusty. Haven't seen you in here for quite a while. Been tearin' around the country with that big rig of yours?"

Rusty grinned. "Sure have, Vicky. Gotta make a living, you know."

Vicky guffawed. "Golly, yes, I'd hate to see a big man like you go hungry." She laughed uproariously. "Let's see, it's a beer for you, and what'll the lady have?"

Rusty looked at Annelise, and she said, "Just coffee, please."

"The lady is Ms. Annelise Kelsey, our new librarian," Rusty said. "Annelise, meet Vicky."

Annelise smiled and said hello. Vicky looked her over. "So you're the gal who drove her car into Rusty's truck. I don't go to the library. Got better things to do than read." She turned to leave. "Be right back with your drinks."

Some of Annelise's distaste for the waitress's rude familiarity must have shown in her face because Rusty put his hand over hers and smiled. "Vicky takes a little getting used to, but she's a good kid."

"She's hardly a kid." The woman had to be at least thirty.

Rusty's smile vanished, and there was censure in his tone. "She's a kid to me. I remember her when she was a scrawny ten-year-old and her mother ran off with another man leaving four children for their father to raise. Unfortunately he wasn't any more interested in them than their mother was, so finally the county took over and put them in foster homes."

Annelise felt awful. "I'm so sorry," she said softly. "I had no right to make snap judgments. I don't usually—it's just…I was wondering…if you think of her as a kid, what must you think of me?''

He squeezed the hand he was holding. "I think you're a beautiful distraction who's sweet and vulnerable and still has a lot of growing up to do.''

"That's not very flattering.''

"Yes it is, honey. Don't you know how tempting that combination can be to a man? Ah, here comes Vicky with our drinks." He sounded relieved.

After more banter between Rusty and the waitress she took their orders and left.

Rusty eyed Annelise's coffee. "Don't you drink?''

She shook her head. "I saw firsthand what liquor can do to a person. I'll never let that happen to me, and it's easier not to acquire the habit than it is to quit.''

"You're not only beautiful and tempting but smart, too." He poured his beer into the glass. "How come you took a position in Raindance? You've apparently lived all your life in Kansas City, and frankly, it usually works the other way around. We lose a lot of our young people to more populated areas—especially those who go away to school—but it's unusual for someone your age with no ties here to move to Raindance from a city. Our population is getting older all the time.''

Annelise put cream in her coffee and stirred it. "I'll admit it wasn't my first choice. My goal is to be a research librarian in one of the country's major libraries, but I need at least a master's for that. Up to now I've gotten by on scholarships and working part-time while I go to school, but I'm burning myself out that way. I decided to take a full-time job and get some experience as well as save money so I can go to graduate school.''

Vicky returned with their soup, and when she left Rusty asked, "But why Raindance? The pay can't be all that great here."

"It's comparable to what I could make as an underling in a city library, and the experience of being head librarian is invaluable. You may not know it, but since Raindance has a regional library that serves a large area it qualifies for a private grant that was set up several years ago by a philanthropist in Lincoln. They can afford to pay me a competitive wage."

"You're right, I didn't know," he said. "But aren't you going to be bored way out here in the sticks? There aren't many people your age in town, and the ones there are married young and have small children."

Annelise shrugged. "I've always been a loner. I never could afford to go out much, and besides I was always too busy. I don't need friends, and I won't be here more than a year—two at the most. I want to finish my education and get on with my career."

Rusty was looking at her with amused indulgence, a look she was familiar with and hated. Why was it that so many men assumed all single women were just marking time until some man married them? She could predict what his next line would be, and she wasn't disappointed.

"What about marriage? How are you going to fit that into your busy schedule?"

She raised her face and let him see the distaste in her wide brown eyes. "I don't ever intend to be dependent on a man, no matter how charming or handsome he is. I certainly won't marry just for the sake of conforming to what's expected of me. But I would like to have children, and with that in mind, if I ever find a man who has a lot of money and shares my desire for a family, I'll consider it."

Rusty looked outraged. "You'd marry for money?"

Annelise tried not to cringe at his accusing tone. "You're damn right I would. My mother married for love, and look what it got her. She came from an upper-middle-class family and had everything she wanted until she met my dad. She was only sixteen, and because Dad was ten years older and was known to drink too much her parents refused to let her go out with him. She was in love and wouldn't listen. Instead, she quit school and they eloped."

Rusty's expression had softened, but by now Annelise was too worked up to care. "My brother was born seven months later, and I came along a couple of years after that. By the time I was ten we'd moved eight times, always to a cheaper rent district. The neighbors were giving us their cast-off clothing, my mom was waiting tables in a greasy spoon for minimum wage and practically no tips, and my grandparents had washed their hands of us. Dad was still technically employed, but he was hung over so much of the time that he missed a lot of work. Since he was a salesman on commission—" she gestured with her hands "—well, you can imagine...."

Rusty nodded, but before he could speak Vicky came with their dinners. When she'd left, Rusty moved closer and took one of Annelise's clenched hands in his. "Where's your brother now?" His tone was filled with tenderness.

"He quit school at seventeen and joined the army. I haven't seen him since. We heard from him once in a while at first, but nothing in the past five years."

Annelise looked up at Rusty and saw the compassion on his face and in his eyes. She didn't want pity. She'd had a lifetime of that and she hated it.

With strength born of determination she sat up straight and pulled her hand from his. "Oh yes, Rusty." Her voice was strong again, too. "You'd better believe that if I ever marry it'll be with dollar signs in my eyes, not stars. My children will never go through what my brother and I did."

Chapter Four

Rusty sat on his oak-trimmed leather sofa with an earthenware mug of steaming coffee in his hand and stared at the television set.

This wasn't the way he'd intended to spend the latter part of the evening, and instead of watching the Kung Fu movie that was showing on the screen his mind wandered back a few hours to the restaurant and Annelise Kelsey.

Ah yes, Annelise. The poor little waif who had literally turned into a woman in his arms. When he'd pulled her out of her wrecked car he'd been so sure she was a teenager, probably a runaway. Most grown women didn't wear long hair in a thick braid down their back.

Damn it, he should have had the sense to steer clear of Annelise when she'd told him the following day that she was twenty-two, but by then he'd been hooked by her helplessness and confusion. He just kept thinking of her as a kid who needed someone to look after her.

With a snort of self-derision he took a swallow of his strong black coffee. He'd found out she was a full-grown woman when he'd kissed her and nearly gone up in smoke—and tonight she'd made it plain that she could and would look after herself very nicely, thank you.

He knew his attitude toward her had cooled after she'd laid out her cold-blooded plans for snaring a rich husband. He couldn't really blame her for her jaded attitude—she'd had a rough time of it—but it scared him to think how easily he could have been caught in her web. Although he'd planned that they'd spend the entire evening together, he'd quickly changed his mind. All he could think of during dinner was taking her home as soon as possible, saying goodbye, and meaning it.

He slammed his mug down on the solid oak coffee table and picked up the remote control to shut off the TV. He knew he'd hurt her by rushing her home with a hurriedly thought-up excuse that she must have known was phony. She'd looked at him with those melting, wide brown eyes, and he'd seen the distress and bewilderment. Instead of taking a little time to say goodnight and thank her for having dinner with him, he'd kissed her lightly on the cheek and beat a hasty retreat.

Damn, he hadn't meant to compound her problems by seeming to reject her, too. He'd had enough psychology classes during his six years at Stanford University to know that she'd think of her father's drinking as a rejection of her and her mother. Children of alcoholics too often felt that they were somehow at fault, that if they were more deserving and lovable the parent would give up the booze and be the sort of father or mother that other kids had.

Logically she no doubt knew that wasn't the case, but emotionally she was still vulnerable.

Unfortunately, so was he. He'd been dangerously susceptible to her ever since that kiss. He'd known that if he ever repeated it he'd be in trouble, but he hadn't suspected the full extent of the danger until she'd inadvertently revealed tonight how contemptuous she was of marriage in general and men in particular. She would use both ruthlessly and without thought of what she might do to the man involved.

Thank the Lord she didn't yet know that his family owned and operated the biggest, most productive ranch in this part of the state. He met her qualifications for a rich husband several times over, but he hoped she'd never find that out.

It was difficult to keep a secret in a small town, but he'd been raised out in the Sandhills on the ranch and had gone to private boarding schools in the eastern part of the state. People in Raindance knew of his background, but they were so used to him as a truck jockey that he doubted they ever thought of him as anything else. He liked the freedom of the open road and traveling around the country, but he had a master's degree in business management and someday soon would start making use of his expensive education and invest in his own trucking company.

He wasn't ready for marriage yet, although eventually he'd settle down and raise a family. Meanwhile he enjoyed his freewheeling life-style and had no intention of letting himself be roped and hog-tied by a child-woman whose only interest in him would be his money.

Annelise spent a restless night trying to figure out what she'd done to make Rusty suddenly become so cool and distant. He'd muttered something about having to see someone about something and taken her home as soon as they'd finished their dinner. She'd tried to get him to come in and visit with Bryce and Carol, but he refused and sprinted off without saying anything about seeing her again.

She'd been looking forward to a good-night kiss, but all she got was a buss on the cheek and a murmured "See ya around." Why had he asked her out in the first place if he couldn't wait to get rid of her?

Worse, why did it matter so much? If she'd inadvertently said or done something to offend him, then he should have told her and given her a chance to apologize or explain. Since he hadn't, she could only assume that because of her dependency on him when she was in the hospital he felt responsible for her, and she was getting to be a burden.

The thought made her feel ill. She didn't want to be a burden on any man, but especially not on Rusty. He'd already done so much for her. She'd behaved so irrationally after the accident, but now she'd have to let him know that she'd recovered fully and no longer needed him—which was absolutely true, she assured herself.

So why did she feel so empty and alone?

The following day, Thursday, Lance came to the library. Annelise saw him come in while she was checking out a stack of mystery novels to a couple of elderly ladies who argued in loud whispers over the merits of guns versus poison as the best way to murder someone.

He stood by the desk and waited until she was finished, then leaned over and said softly, "I've found you a place to live."

She gasped with surprise, then had to remind herself to speak quietly. "Really? That's wonderful. Where?"

He grinned triumphantly. "Have you met Nell and Fred Summers yet?"

Annelise shook her head. "The name doesn't sound familiar."

"They're a retired couple who live across the street and about half a block north of here. Last night their son, who lives in Palm Beach, Florida, called to say that he's being sent to Japan by his firm—I don't remember whether it's cameras or cars—and will be gone for a couple of months. He and his wife are divorced and he has custody of their two teenage kids. He wants Nell and Fred to go to Florida and stay with them while he's gone. Nell came over to tell Mom and was bemoaning the fact that it's such a job to close up the house and drain all the pipes so they won't freeze. I asked her if she'd consider letting you live there and house-sit while they're gone. She thought it was a great idea."

Annelise could hardly keep from shouting with joy. "You mean I'll have a whole house, and it's only half a block from the library?"

Lance seemed almost as excited as she. "Yep. If you're interested they want you to come over as soon as you get off work."

"What do you mean *if* I'm interested?" Her voice reverberated throughout the room, and she promptly lowered it again. "Of course I'm interested! Oh, Lance, I could hug you."

He actually blushed but quickly regained his composure. "That might be a bit difficult with the desk between us," he drawled. "You want I should come back there, or do you want to come out here?"

She giggled like a schoolgirl, but before she could think up a snappy comeback the door opened and several people walked in.

The rest of the day seemed to drag by, but finally it was six o'clock and Lance strode through the door, right on time. She'd already called Bryce to tell him what had happened and that Lance would bring her home after she'd met the Summerses.

When they drove up to the curb and parked, Annelise recognized the house as one Bryce drove past every morning when he took her to work. It was brown stained wood with a glassed-in sun-room across the front and a small three-step-high covered alcove at one side that led to the front door.

Their ring was answered by Fred Summers, a tall, white-haired man, who greeted them and introduced his wife, Nell. Nell was petite, and her brown hair was probably touched up although she had a youthful grace about her that belied the wrinkles in her delicate complexion.

They both seemed delighted that Annelise was willing to stay in their house and look after things. It wasn't a very large place, just two bedrooms and a living room, dining room and kitchen, as well as the sun-room, which was furnished with wicker furniture that gave it a light, airy atmosphere.

Annelise was thrilled, and the Summerses invited her to move in on Sunday so they could show her where everything was before they left the following morning.

Afterward Lance took her to dinner at the Steak and Stein. Again Vicky was the waitress, but she was much more formal and businesslike with Lance than she'd been with Rusty. Come to think of it, Annelise realized, nobody was businesslike with Rusty. He was the open, friendly, big-brother type who was a buddy to everyone.

When Lance escorted Annelise to the Garretts' front door, he refused her invitation to come in but asked her if she'd go out with him on Saturday night. "The Stockmen's Club, a bar on Main Street, features country and western dancing to a live band on Saturday nights," he said. "I'm not awfully good at it, but if you don't mind having your toes stepped on once in a while, I get better as I go along. It's the big excitement on Saturday nights around here, and there's always a crowd."

The idea of going to a dance appealed to Annelise, and she liked Lance. He didn't set her heart pounding and her imagination running wild the way Rusty did, but he was more her type. They shared a lot of the same interests, and they understood each other.

"It sounds like fun," she said, "but I'm warning you, I'm pretty much a novice at country and western dancing. I know the basic steps, but haven't had much practice."

Lance grinned. "Then we should get along great. I'll pick you up about eight-thirty. The ladies wear full skirts or jeans—either's okay."

By the end of the week Rusty hadn't contacted Annelise again, although she couldn't help looking up whenever the library door opened or reaching for the phone when it rang at the Garretts'. She hated the empty feeling of disappointment when it wasn't him, and each time she resolved not to let it happen again—only to break the resolve the next time the door opened or the phone rang.

On Saturday night after dinner she took a quick shower and dressed in jeans and a white, silky Western shirt that Carol had loaned her, trimmed with brightly colored, hand-embroidered flowers on the front and back of the yoke. When Lance arrived he also wore jeans and a Western shirt. Neither wore the regulation cowboy hats, but both donned boots.

The Stockmen's Club was a rectangular building with a bar and tables at the front and a dance floor at the back. It wasn't a club, as the name implied, but a rustic, frontier-style bar with space for dancing. Chairs scraped noisily on the bare plank floors, and the windowless walls had old beer posters tacked on them for decoration.

Annelise frowned. This was the sort of place she'd always avoided. The customers were loud and, if not rowdy, certainly exuberant as the noise level approached more a roar than a hum. She was afraid she'd made a serious mistake by agreeing to come with Lance.

As if reading her mind he took her arm and led her to one of the few empty tables. "I know it's primitive honky-tonk, but that's the way the locals like it. The owner's a straight guy and the place is clean. No backroom gambling or drug dealing, and anyone caught smoking a joint or getting obnoxious from too much booze is thrown out. The cowboys, truckers and young couples come from miles around to cut loose, have a few beers and dance on Saturday nights. Like I said, it's the only show in town."

She smiled as they sat down. "No need to apologize. It's just that I've never been in a place like this before."

Lance signaled to the cocktail waitress. "The band's getting ready to play," he said, nodding in the direction of the bandstand where three men and a woman were tuning up two guitars, a keyboard and a drum.

"Then the crowd will spill out onto the dance floor, too, and we won't be packed in so tight."

The waitress arrived, and Annelise ordered a soft drink. Lance seemed surprised, but then ordered the same. When the barmaid left Annelise looked at him and said, "Just because I don't drink doesn't mean I expect you not to. Please, Lance, feel free to order anything you want."

He smiled and shook his head. "I seldom drink either. Only when I'm with someone else who does. Besides, I'm not familiar enough with the country swing dance steps to remember them if my mind's foggy."

The band began to play, and Annelise and Lance agreed to watch for a while before trying it. The first piece was a rousing one that shook the floor and incited a lot of whooping toward the end. It looked like fun, but in the confined space there was also the possibility of getting trampled if you didn't move fast enough.

The second number was a medium-fast country swing that lent itself to some fancy footwork, and after a few minutes Annelise noticed that the couples were dropping out a few at a time to stand on the sidelines and watch. She mentioned it to Lance, and they got up and walked over to stand against the wall where they could see.

There was now only one couple dancing, and they were definitely exhibition caliber. Annelise immediately recognized Rusty Watt. Who could miss his six-foot-four frame topped by thick mahogany hair that couldn't be completely covered even by his Stetson?

He'd never mentioned that he enjoyed dancing, and for a moment Annelise was too startled to notice his partner. That oversight was corrected almost immedi-

ately because she was nearly as watchable as he, with
soft dark brown hair that fell to her shoulders in a tan-
gle of curls and brushed rhythmically against the lipstick red of her Western-style blouse. With it she wore
a full red, cream and black print skirt that swirled
around her long slender legs and revealed glimpses of a
black petticoat.

Annelise couldn't see her face because the couple
were in constant motion, dipping, twirling, moving together, then apart, while all the time their booted feet
flawlessly executed the four-step in time to the beat of
the music. She would never have believed that a man as
big as Rusty could dance so gracefully, although now
that she thought of it, he walked that way, too.

When the music ended the crowd clapped and
cheered, and Rusty and his partner grinned and bowed.
Obviously this acclamation didn't come as a surprise—
they were used to it. That meant they danced together
often.

Annelise felt as if someone had turned off the sun-
shine in her life and left only the heavy gray of impend-
ing gloom. Was this woman Rusty's love? He'd never
mentioned having a special lady in his life, but then he'd
never said there wasn't one, either.

How could she have been so naive? Of course a man
his age would be involved with someone. It was sur-
prising that he wasn't married. Maybe he had been.
Annelise was appalled to realize how little she actually
knew about him. Come to think of it, she didn't even
know where he lived.

Their meeting and the events following it had been so
traumatic that he'd seemed more like a knight in shining armor than a flesh-and-blood man. Talk about stars
in your eyes! She hadn't even asked about his back-

ground. For her he'd sprung to life full-grown on the dark highway. He had no past and no future, only a present.

A tug on her arm brought her back to her provincial surroundings. "We'd better get back to our table," Lance said, "before someone takes it away from us."

Gratefully she followed him. Rusty hadn't seen her, and she didn't want him to. He might think she was following him around. Their half-finished drinks had apparently warned people that this space was occupied, and Lance and Annelise sank into their chairs while those who had no place to sit surged to the bar.

Lance raised his voice to be heard over the din. "You know Rusty Watt, don't you?"

She nodded, and he continued. "That's right, he was driving the truck that hit your car."

"No," she protested, "I'm the one who hit him. Who's the lady he's with?"

Lance paused. "I'm not sure. I've been away at school so much the past seven years that I've lost track of the people who come and go. I've seen her around town, but I don't know her name or what she does. Maybe she belongs to Rusty. They dance like they've spent a lot of time together."

Annelise set her glass down with a bang. "Didn't they teach you at Harvard that women don't belong to men?" Her annoyance was plain.

Lance grinned. "One of the first things I learned at Harvard was that just by mentioning I was a student there I could have almost any woman I wanted."

Annelise shuddered. "That's disgusting."

He shrugged. "Tell that to the little groupies who hang around the Ivy League colleges."

Before she could think of a suitably cutting remark the music started again, and Lance stood and held out his hand. "Come on, we might as well try it. The best way is just to wade in."

That they did, and Lance proved to be a pretty good dancer. He had a fair command of the steps, and she found it easy to follow him. They were a long way from being as good as Rusty and his partner, but neither did they stumble all over each other. Annelise enjoyed the country beat, and by the second number they were relaxed and having a good time.

It was a short while later during a Texas two-step, a dreamy type of dance, that Annelise began to feel a prickling at the nape of her neck, an uneasy feeling that someone was watching her. At first she ignored it and rested her chin on the hand she'd positioned on Lance's shoulder. The prickling continued, and she was almost sure she was being watched.

She looked up, but everyone in her line of vision was concentrating on his or her own partner. Then Lance whirled them, and her gaze collided with the golden fire of Rusty's hazel eyes. He made no secret of the fact that he was staring at her, or that he didn't like what he was seeing.

She tried for a tentative smile, but he twirled his lady in red away and they were lost in the crowd. With a puzzled sigh she dropped her chin back on Lance's shoulder. Now what had she done to earn her reluctant savior's disfavor? Or was he still upset with her for whatever she'd done on Wednesday? Maybe he was afraid his girlfriend would get the wrong idea about their on-again-off-again friendship.

Back at their table Lance ordered two more colas, and the waitress had just brought them when a male voice behind her set Annelise's heart pounding. "Well, well, this is a surprise. I didn't expect to see you two here together."

It was Rusty, and although his words were friendly enough, Annelise didn't miss the anger underlining them. He had his partner with him, and Lance stood as Rusty introduced them. "Honey, you probably know Lance, here. He's the mayor's son, and this pretty lady with him is Annelise Kelsey, our new librarian. Annelise, I'd like you to meet Maybelle Holden."

They all murmured polite greetings, and Lance invited Rusty and Maybelle to sit down in the two extra chairs. Now that she was across the table from her, Annelise could see that Maybelle had a very pleasing face. It was more round than oval, and her lively green eyes and wide mouth that turned upward in a relaxed natural smile gave the impression of beauty without its actually being a fact.

In spite of her slender figure and carefree appearance there was an air of maturity about Maybelle that convinced Annelise the woman was closer to Rusty's age than her own.

"I should have known you two would get together," Rusty said, "you both being intellectuals and all."

Annelise winced. He was being sarcastic, a side of him she'd never have suspected.

Before either she or Lance could think of a reply, Maybelle spoke. "Rusty's told me about the accident. He said you were pretty banged up, but no one would ever know it now. Are you okay?"

Her voice was husky, sexy but not affectedly so, and it held genuine concern.

"I'm fine, thanks to Rusty's quick action in getting me to the hospital and seeing that I had good care. I'm afraid I was a real bother to him."

"It's a good thing I didn't get hooked on playing 'uncle,'" Rusty said, "'cause you sure don't need me anymore." There was a grin on his face, but his tone had a cutting edge. "You should have told me how well you can take care of yourself. It would have saved me from wondering if I was going to have to adopt you."

Annelise blinked at his deliberate cruelty. What was the matter with him? He'd never treated her with anything but tenderness and respect, but in the past few days he'd dumped her unceremoniously on her doorstep and disappeared without a word. Now he was acting as if it were all her fault, as if she was the one who'd done the dumping.

While she was still recovering, the music started again, and Rusty looked at Lance. "How about changing partners this time? I've never danced with my little foundling."

Lance glanced at her and stammered, "Well, I...um..."

Before he could finish the sentence Rusty grabbed her hand and pulled her up. "Come on, honey, show Uncle Rusty how they do it in Kansas City."

Annelise sputtered as he practically dragged her to the dance floor. He was being rude, chauvinistic and deliberately belittling, and she didn't like it one bit. "Let go of me," she hollered above the noise that seemed to be a permanent part of the atmosphere. "I'm not a child, and I'm certainly not 'yours.'"

"That's for sure," he growled as he pulled her into his arms and led her onto the floor. "Any woman of mine will be warm and loving, not a scheming little gold digger.''

"What!" Annelise was so dumbfounded by his brutal description of her that she stopped dancing and he stumbled over her.

Without missing more than a couple of beats he put both arms around her and lifted her feet off the floor, then held her close against him as he continued moving to the rhythm. She threw both her arms around his neck to maintain her balance. Even though she was five-foot-five, he was still nearly a foot taller and outweighed her by almost a hundred pounds.

"You didn't lose any time zeroing in on the richest young bachelor in town, did you?" His anger was undisguised now. "Hell, I leave you alone for a couple of days and you've already picked out a willing victim."

"What!" She knew she was repeating herself, but she couldn't believe what she was hearing.

"Your conversation's deteriorated," he snapped. "Have you convinced Lance to marry you yet? You better understand right now that I'm not going to allow this. Lance is a nice kid. A bit of a nerd, but nice, and I won't let you use him."

By now Annelise was totally confused, although she realized what he was ranting about had something to do with her statement that she'd only marry a rich man.

She pounded on his shoulders. "Put me down. I don't know what you're talking about, but I don't have to stay here and be insulted."

His hold on her tightened. "I don't see that you've got much choice, do you? You're going to listen to what I have to say."

He lowered her feet to the floor where she had to dance or be run over. She chose the former and followed his lead as he kept her prisoner in his arms and continued the conversation. "I gave you credit for at least having the decency to pick a man who was sophisticated enough to know what he was getting into when you set out to find a rich husband, but I was wrong. You don't have any intention of playing fair, do you? You'll tear the heart out of a boy like Lance Farr."

The music stopped, and Annelise pushed with all her strength against Rusty's broad, hard chest in an effort to break his hold on her, but it had no effect at all. "Damn you, let me go," she stormed. "You have no right to make snap decisions about me. You're not my uncle or my big brother, and it's none of your business who I go out with or why."

The music started again, and Rusty kept both arms around her as he once more moved to the rhythm. "It's not you I'm worried about—it's Lance," he said. "The poor kid's always been something of a misfit. Too damn bright for this town. The kids teased him because he was small and wore glasses and knew all the answers to the teachers' questions. His parents didn't help. His dad tried to make a 'man' of him by insisting he go out for sports, and his mother was overprotective of her 'baby.' He grew up a loner. No friends, either boys or girls. Even the adults, some of them his teachers, resented him because he was smarter than they were."

Annelise had guessed at most of this, but hearing it confirmed by Rusty was doubly poignant. How could he think she'd do anything to hurt Lance? Anyway, it would be years before she was ready to marry.

Some of her anger faded, although she was still hurt by Rusty's attitude. "Look, Rusty," she said in a placating tone, "I'm not going to hurt Lance—he's my friend."

"A guy like him needs more than a friend for a wife," he interrupted. "He needs someone who'll love him for himself, not just for his money. He needs a woman who is as naive and somewhat bewildered by the world as he. A woman who will accept him for what he is, not for what he has."

They were dancing easily now, and Annelise no longer had to think about the steps in order to do them. "I'm sure he does, but—"

"And you need a man who'll take charge and see to it that you grow up and come to terms with the real world," he interrupted, seemingly unaware that she'd spoken. "You've read Cinderella too many times. Believe me, there aren't any Prince Charmings out there with a glass slipper just waiting for a princess to fit into it. There are only men, with faults and insecurities and farfetched dreams."

If it hadn't meant missing a step Annelise would have stamped her foot, preferably on top of his. "Don't tell me I need a man! You're the one who should come to terms with the 'real world.' You're thirty years behind the times. What I need is to finish my education so I won't ever have to rely on anybody for anything."

Rusty's short laugh was taunting. "I suppose you're going to tell me it's only coincidence that the first guy you date in Raindance just happens to be the only one who's young, unmarried and *rich*. Come on, give me credit for a little intelligence."

"Why should I? You're acting like an idiot."

He raised one eyebrow rakishly. "Oh? Well let me tell you something, Miss Know-It-All, there's a lot more to marriage than having babies. In order to make them you have to get pretty doggone intimate with their father, and I don't think you have a clue as to what making love is all about. I'll bet you've never even been kissed properly."

She gasped at his audacity, then promptly stumbled and wound up crushed against the long length of him as he sought to steady her. "You're being crude," she grated. "You had me fooled. I thought you were a gentleman."

They were in a corner close to the outside wall, and she slowly realized that instead of dancing they were standing still with their arms around each other. "My innocent little virgin," he said huskily, "You don't want to be made love to by a gentleman. What you need is someone who can match your fire. Come on, I'll prove it to you."

He took her hand and pulled her over to a door that she hadn't noticed before. "Let go of me," she said as she struggled to release her hand. "Where are you going?"

He opened the door, and a gust of cold early November air blew in. "Rusty, it's cold out there!" she squealed, as he tugged her through and closed it behind him.

They were in a narrow deserted alley at the back of the building, and the only illumination was a full moon and a sky strewn with stars. "I'll keep you warm," he growled, and lifted her off the ground as he took her in his arms and leaned against the rough wall.

Caught off balance, she again threw her arms around his neck and started to protest, but before she could his mouth lowered to cover hers, and her half-formed words died aborning.

It was like the first time all over again, the awakening that quickened her whole body. All thought of resistance fled as her arms tightened and her lips yielded to his. She felt his hand at the back of her head, and the kiss became insistent. She wanted to respond more fully, to give him what he was seeking, but she didn't know how.

Her breasts were squashed against his chest, and she was sure he could feel her heart hammering. It was sending blood pounding through her veins and making her breathing choppy as she stroked her fingers through his hair and toppled his Stetson.

Neither seemed to notice the loss. Instinctively she tipped her head to one side to give him access to the long line of her throat, and his mouth left hers to caress the fragrant silk of her skin and the throbbing pulses at the underside of her jaw.

She moaned with pleasure as tickling pinpricks raced up and down her spine, and then his lips took hers again. As the tip of his tongue outlined her lips she tensed, then sighed softly as they parted slightly. Carefully he invaded further, exploring the soft underside of her upper lip, and her straight, even teeth. No one had ever done that to her before, and after the first surprise she put her hands on either side of his head and held him there so he'd know she wanted him to continue.

She'd forgotten the cold, and the music, and even Lance and Maybelle waiting for them inside. One of his hands wandered over her back to the indentation of her waist and came to rest on her firm, round buttocks. She shivered but not with cold, and as she pressed even closer she felt the physical evidence of his pulsating need.

It was then that he dragged his mouth from hers and buried his face in the side of her neck. "Annelise!" It was little more than a ragged whisper. "You didn't tell me you were a witch who casts spells on men. My God, what are you doing to me?"

She swallowed in an effort to dampen her dry mouth. "I believe you were showing me how a real man kisses." Her voice wasn't in any better shape than his.

"I didn't expect to be poleaxed in the process," he muttered, and kissed her again, hard and long and hungrily, before he put her down, grabbed for her wrist and strode back into the dance hall, once more pulling her along behind him.

Chapter Five

On Sunday Annelise packed her belongings, and late that afternoon Lance arrived to take her to the Summerses' house.

As he and Bryce stowed her luggage in the trunk, Annelise turned to Carol and her throat choked up with emotion. How could she ever thank this warm and thoughtful woman for taking her in when she'd had no place to go? Carol had been friend and adviser when Annelise needed both so desperately. If she tried to say these things Annelise knew she'd break down and cry. Finally she just threw her arms around the other woman and murmured, "I love you."

She did the same with Bryce, and he hugged her back. "It's been our pleasure to have you with us," he assured her hoarsely while Carol wiped tears from her magnificent blue eyes.

Lance looked away and shifted from one foot to the other in embarrassment, then breathed a sigh that could only be relief when he finally got Annelise in the car and drove away.

It was a bright, sunny afternoon, warm for November, and several of the neighbors on North Main Street were in their yards as Lance and Annelise drove up in front of the Summers home and began to unload her suitcases. Next door a pretty blond woman was chasing after a laughing, towheaded toddler who skidded off course and ran smack into Annelise. She picked her up and held the squirming little body until the mother reached them.

The woman was laughing, too, as she held out her arms to her daughter. "Sorry," she said breathlessly as she took the child. "This little one's going to make an old woman of me before my time. I'd like to get my hands on the joker who said girls were easy to raise." She hugged the little girl, then returned her attention to Annelise. "You must be Annelise Kelsey. Carol Garrett told me you'd be our neighbor. I'm Rosemarie Perkins, and this little whirlwind is our daughter, Misty. Welcome to the neighborhood."

Annelise knew she'd found another friend. "Thank you. Carol told me about you, too. She said you've known each other all your lives and were in the same grade in school."

"That's right—she's the closest thing I'll ever have to a sister," Rosemarie said as she turned toward her own house, still juggling the bouncing child. "We'll have you over for dinner as soon as you've settled in," she called over her shoulder as she walked away. "My husband, Jim, is anxious to meet you. Hi, Lance, you're invited, too."

* * *

A week went by without any sign of Rusty. Not a phone call, a visit or even a casual meeting on the street. After that searing kiss Annelise had been sure he'd get in touch with her, but as the days went by she realized that once again she'd read more into it than she should have.

She hated being such an innocent. If only she'd had more experience. She'd missed the give and take of teenage flirtations, and now she was out of her depth with adult men.

What did Rusty want of her? Did he expect something she wasn't providing? Was he just toying with her? Even if he was, there didn't seem to be anything she could do about it. Her good sense simply deserted her where he was concerned. Every time she saw him she wanted to throw her arms around him, and when he held her she melted. She was setting herself up for heartbreak of monumental proportions if she didn't get control of her emotions.

She should have realized Saturday night when he'd hauled her so unceremoniously back into the dance hall, left her at the table with Lance and taken off with Maybelle that he'd just been amusing himself with her, but she'd been shaken to the core of her being by that hot, sensual, intense kiss.

When he'd cupped her bottom with his hands and pushed her so intimately against him she'd simply ignited, and he'd certainly been aroused. He hadn't tried to disguise or deny that, yet a few minutes later he'd calmly walked away with his date without even saying thank you or good night.

Obviously she'd made a fool of herself again. Not only had she not tried to repel his amorous attack, she'd actually encouraged it. Also she'd treated Lance shabbily. Even though he didn't know about her behavior with Rusty, it was unforgivable of her to go out with one man and then let another man kiss her. Especially when Lance was behaving like such a gentleman.

Now it was Sunday again, and she'd been living in the house for a week. What a marvelous feeling to be on her own, to be able to come and go as she pleased without upsetting anyone else's schedule.

Annelise still felt a lingering concern for her mother, but they talked on the phone every Sunday, and today Sandra Kelsey had told her daughter that she'd been accepted into an adult education program to train as a medical assistant and be paid a stipend while she was learning. After all, she was only forty-one, and for the first time since she'd quit high school to get married she, like Annelise, had only herself to take care of. It seemed that she was going to pick up the pieces and make the most of the life ahead of her. Annelise was jubilant.

It had been a peaceful day. Since the churches and their activities were an integral part of the social life of the town, Annelise had taken to going with Bryce and Carol when she was staying with them. Now it was an easy three-and-a-half-block walk, and she was continuing the practice. After the services Rosemarie and Jim Perkins had invited her to have midday dinner with them and their family. Jim was a nice-looking sandy-haired man who obviously adored his wife and three small children.

At a few minutes before six, Annelise went into the kitchen to fix herself a cup of hot chocolate before settling down to watch the evening news, but she'd just opened the refrigerator when the doorbell rang. Before she could get from the kitchen to the small entryway it had rung several more times—short, angry blasts as though someone were jabbing at it.

"I'm coming, for heaven's sake," she called, and pulled open the heavy door only to stand blinking with surprise.

It was Rusty who stood on the other side of the glass, and he didn't look happy. "I want to talk to you," he muttered.

"Well, hello, it's nice to see you, too," she said, the sarcasm heavy in her tone.

He pulled the storm door open without waiting for an invitation and strode inside, then stood looking around the cozy living room while she shut the doors behind him. A fire crackled in the fireplace, and that and the reading lamp beside the blue upholstered swivel rocker in the corner illuminated the area with a soft, romantic glow.

He turned to her and glared. "Is it true that Lance Farr got this place for you?"

"Well, yes.... That is, he—"

"And did he move you in the day after you were together at The Stockmen's Club?"

He was throwing questions at her so fast she couldn't think. "Yes, but—"

He looked about ready to explode as he stamped away from her and shrugged out of his sheepskin-lined denim jacket. "Damn it, Annelise, I've said before that you need a keeper, and since nobody else has come forward, I'll volunteer. I told you I wouldn't stand for this, and I meant it." He tossed the jacket over a wingback chair.

Annelise's mouth dropped open and she stared. He was at it again, making totally unfounded accusations.

The man was demented! He didn't even make sense. "I don't know what you're talking about," she protested.

"The hell you don't. Do the Summerses know that you and the mayor's son are using their house for a love nest? What's the matter, couldn't you talk him into marrying you? Did you decide to give him a preview of what the honeymoon would be like?"

She could only continue to stare as he continued. "Let me tell you that's not very smart. He'll just sample the goodies and run. If you knew anything at all about men you'd know that you have to keep them wanting."

The rage that had built up in her was almost more than she could handle as she walked over to stand beside him. "Lean down a little, Rusty," she said, and was amazed at how calm she sounded.

He looked startled, then bent toward her as though he thought she wanted to reach up and touch him. She did, but not quite the way he'd expected. She clenched her fist, pulled back her arm and hit him in the jaw with all the strength she could muster.

Caught totally off guard, he stumbled sideways, losing his Stetson and knocking over the chair before he managed to steady himself. His hand went up to cover his cheek, and he glared at her in shocked amazement. "Why, you little—!" With one swift movement he grabbed her, lifted her off the floor and held her with both huge hands spanning her waist.

She pounded on his chest with her fists. "You bastard!" she shouted. "Who do you think you are that you can call me a—a—"

"Watch your language, little lady," he said tersely. He stood her back on the floor but continued to hold her. "You're the one who's calling names."

"It serves you right. You force your way in here and manhandle me—"

"*I* manhandled *you*!" He shouted back. "That blow you landed probably loosened my back teeth, and my jaw'll be swollen for a week." He took one hand away from her waist and rubbed his cheek. "Where did you learn to pack such a wallop?"

"I worked nights most of the time I was in school, and the neighborhood we lived in was rough. I learned to protect myself. What gives you the right to come storming in here and accuse me of sleeping with Lance? You're not my father." She was shaking with fury.

"Thank God for small favors," he muttered. "Do you deny that you and Lance are lovers?"

"Of course I deny it, and where did you ever get such a ridiculous idea? I haven't seen or heard anything from you. If you're so sure I'm living in sin why have you waited so long to protest? I've been on my own for a whole week." The hand she'd hit him with began to throb, and she rubbed it with the other one.

"I've been gone," Rusty said, with considerably less heat than before. "I work for a living, you know. I got back late this afternoon, and that's when I heard the gossip—"

"Gossip!" She planted her hands on her hips and glared at him. "I'll bet you heard it in a bar, didn't you?"

He had the grace to look sheepish. "Well, yeah, but—"

Most of her rage drained away and was replaced by a cold, empty sense of despair. She slumped and turned away from him. "Your faith and high opinion of me are touching." Her tone was bleakly sarcastic. "Please leave, Rusty. If you're willing to judge my actions on the gossip of a bunch of drunks in a saloon then I don't want to see you anymore. I don't need friends like that."

She heard him catch his breath, and then felt his hands cup her shoulders. "I'm sorry, honey," he said raggedly. "You're right, I am a bastard, but they weren't drunks, just local businessmen relaxing at The Stockmen's Club who knew I'd been gone and were bringing me up-to-date on the latest news."

He must have felt her stiffen because his hands tightened on her, and he hastened to continue. "Okay, you're right, it was gossip, not news, but they were just speculating, not accusing. That was my own interpretation. I don't like to admit it, even to myself, but I was wild, crazy jealous."

She looked over her shoulder and up at him, surprise written all over her face. "Yeah, I know," he said with a sheepish grin, "I had no right, and I was as surprised as you are, but the more I thought about it the madder I got and . . . well, I guess my temper goes with the red in my hair, but when it's roused I don't stop and think, I act. I'm not proud of it, and I truly am sorry. Please say you'll forgive me."

His tone was contrite, but her mind snagged on the words *wild, crazy jealous* and clung to them. Rusty was jealous of her relationship with Lance!

She turned around to face him, and for the first time noticed that the whole side of his face where she'd hit him was flaming red. The last of her anger faded and was replaced with regret. "I—I'm sorry," she stammered. "I should have hit you with my open hand instead of my fist."

He had a pained look as he put his palm to his jaw and moved it back and forth. "Somehow I don't think that would have made a whole lot of difference," he said, but there was a touch of amusement in his tone. "Just remind me never to lean down for you again."

She felt awful. He was so big, and she'd been so mad that for a minute she'd really wanted to hurt him. He deserved to be slapped, but she'd overreacted. She'd known he couldn't, wouldn't, hit her back.

Carefully she put her hand up and touched the bruise. "I'm—I'm really sorry," she stammered, and realized that her lips were trembling. "I'd better get you some ice."

She found an ice bag in the bathroom closet and filled it while Rusty watched. "Here," she said, and handed it to him. "Hold this against your cheek."

He took the bag with one hand and put his other arm around her waist. "Okay, but let's go sit in the living room, and you can tell me about you and young Farr."

For a moment she stiffened with resistance. She didn't owe him any explanations. He was the one who'd come charging in like an angry bull and ...

The defiance died as quickly as it had sprung to life. She didn't want to quarrel with Rusty, and if he cared enough about her to be upset because of his mistaken assumption about her relationship with Lance then she should be grateful. None of the other men in her life— her father, grandfather or big brother—had loved her enough to set aside their own weaknesses or prejudices and worry about her.

They sat down on the sofa, and Rusty cuddled her against him with one arm while he held the ice pack to his face with the other hand. "Okay," he said, "now what's with you and Lance?"

She drew a deep breath. "The only thing between us is friendship. Lance is a nice guy and, as you pointed out earlier, a misunderstood one. I like him, and he seems to like me. We've gone out together a few times, and he was thoughtful enough to arrange for me to house-sit for the Summerses while they're visiting their son's family in Florida.''

"House-sit?"

"Yes, they were worried about leaving the place shut up during the cold winter months, and Lance told them I needed somewhere to live. It's a mutual agreement. I don't pay rent, and they don't pay me to stay here.''

Rusty's fingers moved absently over her waist and stomach, starting a clamor in her nervous system. "Do you swear that you're not setting him up to be your rich, and unloved, husband?''

She sighed. "I'm not obliged to swear anything to you, but I'll tell you that I have no intention of marrying Lance. We don't have that kind of relationship, and besides, neither of us is ready to get married yet. And I darn well take exception to your insistence that my rich husband will be 'unloved.' I couldn't marry a man I didn't love, it's just that it won't be the wildly passionate lust that turns women into slaves. It will be a mature, quiet, friendly kind of love.''

Rusty grunted. "The poor sucker can get that kind of affection from his dog and still keep his freedom."

Annelise sat up and tried to push away from him, but he dropped the ice pack and put both arms around her, pinning her to him. "Darn it, Rusty," she grated through clenched teeth, "you aren't even trying to understand what I'm saying. How did you get to be such an authority on love, anyway? You're thirty-six years old and, as far as I know, have never had a wife or children.'' When he didn't refute her statement she continued. "At least I'm not afraid of making a commitment, which is more than you seem to have done."

For a moment he rested his chin on top of her head and said nothing, just held her close while her anger once more drained away. She seemed to be incapable of staying mad at this baffling man, even though he kept her in constant turmoil.

"I'm afraid you've got a point there," he said. "It's true, I'm not anxious to give up my independence. I like coming and going as I please without having to report in to anybody. It's a great feeling to work when I want to, play when I feel like it and go where the mood strikes. Being responsible for nobody but myself saves me from a lot of stress, and I'm not ready to give that up, but one of the reasons is that I've never yet found a woman I wanted to spend the rest of my life with. Damned if I'm going to arbitrarily track down a maternally inclined female and marry her just so she'll have my babies."

He picked up the ice bag he'd dropped on the sofa when she'd tried to pull away and put it back to his face, all the while holding her close with his other arm. "I want more than that," he continued. "I want a woman I can love, one who'll love me even more than she loves our children."

Annelise's heart sped up, and a picture flashed in her mind. A portrait of her feeding a baby with mahogany-colored curls at her breast and Rusty proudly looking on.

She closed her eyes and burrowed her face into his massive flannel-shirted chest in an effort to shut out the unwelcome image. No! Not her! She wasn't going to fall in love with an undereducated truck driver who drank beer and hung out in cheap saloons to listen to hillbilly music.

She felt Rusty's arm tighten around her and heard the ice pack slide to the couch as he stroked his fingers through her long unbound hair with the other hand. "Hey there." He sounded disturbed. "What's the matter, honey?"

He held her head gently against his chest, and she was immediately and profoundly ashamed of her snobbish thoughts. Rusty was the dearest person in the whole world, and any woman would be proud to be his wife. It's just that she wanted a different type of man for a husband.

So why did she feel warm and comfortable and dreamy with her head cradled on his chest and his arms holding her so close?

It was definitely time to change the subject. "I'm all right," she said in answer to his question. "Rusty, you know everything about me, but I don't know anything about you. Tell me about yourself. Are your parents still alive? Do you have brothers and sisters? I don't even know where you live."

He didn't answer right away, and when he did he was anything but effusive. "Yeah, my parents are still alive, and I have two brothers. They all live on a ranch in the Sandhills south of town."

"You mean they all work for the same rancher?"

Again he hesitated. "Something like that."

She waited a minute, expecting him to explain, but when he didn't she asked, "What do they do?"

"Do?" He sounded puzzled.

"You know, what do they do on the ranch? Is your mother the housekeeper?"

"Mmm..."

She didn't know whether that meant yes or no, but since he didn't correct her she continued. "And your dad? Is he the ranch manager, or—"

"Mmm..."

Annelise sighed with exasperation and sat up, although still within the circle of his arms. "Rusty, for heaven's sake, if you don't want to talk about your family just say so. I'm not trying to pry secrets out of you, I just want to get to know you better."

For a moment their glances connected, then he leaned down and kissed her on the tip of her nose. "I doubt that I could have any secrets from you, my little inquisitor," he said wryly. "All you have to do is curl that soft, lush body against me, and I'll tell you anything you want to know. Mom takes care of the house, Dad manages the ranch, and my two brothers do whatever has to be done."

She let him settle her against his chest again. "You mean they're ranch hands?"

He chuckled softly. "Yeah, they're ranch hands all right, but they might take exception if you called them that to their faces."

She had the distinct feeling that he was laughing at her, or at least at what she was saying, but she hadn't the faintest idea why. Again she sat up, her brow creased with perplexity. "I don't understand. Did I say something wrong?"

His amusement vanished and he shook his head. "No, of course not. It's just a family joke. Jack's forty-two and the oldest. He and his wife, Hannah, have four kids. Bud's forty, and he has a wife, Peggy, and three sons."

Annelise sighed. "It must be nice to have a large family like that. How come you don't work on the ranch, too?"

He guided her head back down to his chest. "I prefer driving the truck. I like the open road, the comradery of the other drivers, the gypsy life-style."

Annelise fastened her arms around his waist. "Don't you ever wish you'd gone to college? It's still not too late, you know. You did get good grades in high school, didn't you?"

She felt him stiffen, and during the long silence that followed she wished she'd never brought the subject up. Maybe he hadn't been able to afford to go away to school.

When he spoke his tone was biting. "Yes, Annelise, I got passing grades in high school, but did it ever occur to you that it's possible to make a good living and be happy without a university degree? A big percentage of the people in this country manage to bumble through without ever setting foot in a college classroom. They work, marry, have children and die without the help of a piece of paper that tells the world they spent four years in the hallowed halls of some institute of higher learning. A hell of a lot of them are a damn sight happier than the Ph.D. who sits in his ivory tower and contemplates his navel, and I think it's about time you understood that."

Annelise was stricken by his verbal attack, and all the more so because she knew she deserved it. She hadn't meant to demean him, but that's the way it had sounded. His education, or lack of it, was none of her business, and by bringing the subject up she'd as much as told him she was better than he because she'd had more schooling.

A hot wave of shame washed over her, and she raised her flaming face to look at him. "Oh, Rusty, I didn't mean to imply—"

The expression on his face was cold and foreboding. "Maybe not," he interrupted, not giving her a chance to apologize, "but that regal attitude of yours is getting tiresome. I'm approaching middle age, and I like my life just the way it is. I don't intend to change it for anyone, especially a kid who's still wet behind the ears and has delusions of grandeur because she's spent four years in college."

His words were like whiplashes, and she winced as each one lacerated her tender ego. "Rusty! Please. I'm sorry. I wasn't criticizing you, I—"

He put his hands on her arms and pulled them from around his waist, then set her away from him and stood up. "No, I don't suppose you were," he said, more gently this time, "but it sounded like it. You'd better learn to think before you speak, Annelise, because most of the folks in this town are good old country farm stock. The majority of them don't have college educations. They're home and family people, and their favorite entertainment is watching sitcoms on television. The few times they go to the city it's to see the Cornhuskers play football, not to attend the opera or ballet. They're good, hard-working, reliable people, so either learn to accept them the way they are or find a job somewhere else."

He picked his hat up off the floor and jammed it on his head, then retrieved his jacket from the chair and pulled it on as he strode toward the front door with Annelise right behind him. "Rusty. Please don't leave. At least let me apologize...."

He pulled the door open, then turned back to look at her. "We've both said more than enough for one night. I don't think either of us needs to continue this conversation."

He stamped out and shut the door behind him.

Annelise leaned heavily against the wall in the small entryway when her knees threatened to buckle. She was deeply ashamed, which seemed to be a consistently recurring state for her lately. What on earth had gotten into her? Usually she was tactful almost to a fault, but since she'd met Rusty Watt every time she opened her mouth she uttered something to offend him.

Putting her hands to her burning face she fought back the urge to sob. He was right, she'd been way out of line in telling him he should go back to school. He'd been a grown man for a long time now, and he was certainly old enough to know what sort of life he wanted. He probably made good wages trucking, and he obviously enjoyed it. Who was she to imply that it wasn't a classy enough occupation for him? In her own family her father had been a drunk, her mother a scrubwoman and her brother, a high-school dropout!

She flexed her legs and slid slowly down the wall until she was sitting on the floor with her arms around her shins and her head buried in her upraised knees. She couldn't bear it that Rusty had such a low opinion of her. If he'd only stayed and let her explain. It might not have changed the way he felt, but at least he may have understood that she hadn't been deliberately insulting.

The antique clock on the sideboard in the dining room bonged nine times, and Annelise lifted her head. Nine o'clock. It was still early enough for her to go after Rusty and apologize. If she didn't do it tonight she'd never be able to sleep. Then it struck her that she didn't know where he lived, and even if she could find out she had no way to get there.

She stood up and walked toward the telephone. That old excuse wouldn't wash. Carol could tell her his address, and Raindance wasn't so big that she couldn't walk anywhere within its radius. She wouldn't dream of being out alone on foot at night in Kansas City, but she would be safe enough here where everyone knew everyone else.

She phoned the Garrett residence, and Carol gave her directions to Rusty's house. Annelise was surprised to find that it was only three blocks east and half a block south of her. She thought about calling to make sure he was home, but knew he'd tell her not to come if she did. Instead she changed into her gray wool slacks and a heavy heather-colored sweater, put on her quilted parka and left the house.

It was only then that she realized how cold it had gotten. The day had been sunny and chilly but not uncomfortably so. Now the temperature had dropped substantially, and the earlier breeze had become a biting wind that lowered the chill factor even more.

As she walked she reached up to put the hood of her jacket over her head, but she was heading into the wind and the hood wouldn't stay on unless she held it in place. Unfortunately she'd rushed off without her gloves, and her bare hands were freezing.

Even though she sped up to a jogging pace it seemed to take forever before she came to Rusty's street and turned south. She was out of breath and panting by the time she approached the middle of the block and spotted the big old cottonwood tree Carol had mentioned as a landmark. To her relief she saw there were lights on in the house behind it. Thank heavens, Rusty was home!

It was too dark to get a good look at the house, but she was grateful that the roofed porch was protected from the wind as she stood there searching for the doorbell. When she realized there wasn't one she banged on the door with the small cold fist that still ached from the blow she'd landed on his iron jaw.

She could hear footsteps coming. A man as big as Rusty didn't walk softly, and she could trace his course from the back of the house to the front. The porch light went on just seconds before the door opened and he was silhouetted on the other side of the glass. "Good Lord, what are you doing here?" he said, and pushed the storm door open.

He reached out and took her hand to help her in. "Your hands are like ice!" he scolded. "How did you get here?"

Stepping out onto the porch he looked around as if expecting to see a car waiting for her.

"I walked," she answered.

"In the dark and the cold?" He came in and shut the doors, then took her arm and led her to the tall, slender heat vent on the wall in the living room.

The blast of warm air felt heavenly as Rusty stood in front of her and placed her chilled hands in the middle of his chest on the soft flannel of his shirt and covered them with his own. "You little idiot," he said softly. "Why didn't you phone and ask me to come after you? Surely you know better than to walk around alone at night."

"I—I was afraid you'd s-s-say you didn't want me...." she answered through chattering teeth.

A low moan escaped him as he wrapped her in his arms. "Don't want you!" His voice was hoarse with tension, and he rubbed his still-red cheek against her cold one. "Oh, my little love, haven't you figured out yet that it's because I want you so much that I've been behaving like a madman?"

Chapter Six

Annelise melted into Rusty's embrace and sighed as the anguish she'd been feeling vanished and was replaced by a surge of joy, slightly tempered by disbelief. "That's not exactly the impression you've given me," she murmured.

"God, you're such a little innocent." He spoke with a mixture of approval and resentment. "That's what's driving me up the wall. I want to protect that innocence and ravish it with equal urgency. You're making a shambles of my libido, and it's damned frustrating."

Annelise didn't know how to respond. She was having the same problem. Not that Rusty was innocent— far from it, a man as sexy as he was had probably had his share of women. But for the first time in Annelise's life she felt the heady, nagging, insistent desire to explore the mysteries of lovemaking.

Unfortunately, somewhere along the way she'd acquired the strong conviction that making love and making a commitment were one and the same. Deep in her soul she knew that she could never have the one without the other, and a man like Rusty had no place in her life except as a lover. They were poles apart and totally incompatible in every other way.

But, oh, he made her feel so good! From the first moment there on the side of the road he'd warmed her and protected her and cared about her, and she was bound to him with invisible bands that would stretch but seemed unbreakable.

At last she raised her head and looked up at him. His jaw was swollen—not much, but she knew it must still hurt. She raised her hand and cupped the bruised area. "Oh, Rusty, I'm sorry I hit you so hard. I honestly didn't know I had that much strength." She stroked him gently. "Can you ever forgive me?"

He turned his head slightly and kissed her palm. "There's nothing to forgive; I had it coming. I just hope you can forgive me for behaving like such a jackass, not once but twice in the same evening."

"I deserved it the second time," she said sadly. "Do you suppose you could trust me enough to lean down again? This time I want to kiss your jaw, not hit it."

He hugged her close. "I have a better idea. How about if we get you out of this heavy jacket and go sit together on the couch. I'll be putting myself totally at your mercy then, which should prove that I trust you."

He'd unzipped the parka while he was talking, and now he pulled the sleeves off her arms, one at a time, and tossed it across a chair.

It was only then that Annelise's attention focused on her surroundings, and she saw that they were in a medium-sized room furnished and decorated in early bachelor-digs decor. The walls were oyster white, but

had probably acquired the slight gray tinge from age
rather than design. A faded rose flowered carpet that
had obviously been donated from somebody's attic was
centered in the middle of the hardwood floor, and the
windows were covered with slatted blinds but no curtains.

The furniture was another matter. The three main
pieces, a massive sofa, easy chair with ottoman and a
separate recliner, were thickly upholstered, covered with
heavy maroon leather and monstrously expensive by
anyone's standards. The effect was offset, however, by
two identical beat-up lamp tables and a matching coffee table with numerous round stains, probably from
beer cans, soaked into the wood; the tables, no doubt,
were also someone's cast-off rejects.

She wasn't aware Rusty had been watching her until
he spoke. "It's not fancy, but I'm on the road most of
the time and only touch base here now and then."

She glanced up quickly, wondering if she'd offended
him again, but he was still grinning. "It's a very nice
house," she said, and meant it. It was small but warm
and comfortable.

The sofa was positioned under the wide, multipaned
front window, and they sat down side by side. It was
every bit as comfortable as it looked, and she sighed
with pleasure as Rusty put his arm around her and said
quietly, "You promised me a kiss."

Not only were his legs long, but so was his body, and
even sitting down it was difficult for Annelise to reach
his left cheek from the right side. Bringing her legs up
she knelt beside him, then put her arms lightly around
his shoulders and leaned over to kiss the discolored
swelling on his jaw. She touched it tenderly and repeat-

edly with her lips while she stroked his cheek and temple with the soft pads of her fingers.

He relaxed against her, and she guided his head to the valley between her breasts and held him. She wondered if he could feel her heart pound as she settled her chin on the top of his head and continued to caress his jaw with her fingers. "Does it feel better now?" she asked.

"Honey," he murmured contentedly, "if I felt any better I'd know I'd died and gone to heaven. Feel free to punch me out anytime if you'll guarantee that we'll wind up like this afterward."

Annelise moved her hand around to massage the tight muscles at the back of his neck and shoulders. "You're all knotted up," she said as she felt him start to unwind.

"It's been a rough week." His tone was ragged with exhaustion. "I've hardly been out of that truck except for a fifteen-hour layover in New Orleans. I parked it, took a taxi into town to a hotel with a king-size bed and crashed."

"But surely you don't drive day and night!"

He chuckled. "No, that's against the law. My cab has a sleeper. I pull into one of the big truck stops and snooze for a few hours at a time, but it's too small and cramped for a man my size. I got into Omaha about noon today, and then drove on home after I'd delivered my freight. I parked the tractor at the garage where I keep it, picked up the Bronco and stopped at the bar before coming on to the house. That's when I heard about you and Lance. I promptly started breathing smoke and fire, and the next thing I knew I was raging at you like a lunatic. It's just as well that you hit me before I made an even bigger ass of myself."

She bent her head and again trailed kisses along his sore cheek while continuing to rub his nape and shoulders. "You shouldn't push yourself so hard," she whispered against his ear. "Why didn't you stay over in Omaha and get some rest?" She took his lobe between her teeth and sucked gently.

He caught his breath and brought one hand up to fondle her breast through the bulky sweater. "I was in a hurry. I needed to touch base with you again."

He said it so simply, but now she knew what a "leaping heart" felt like. Her own had just executed the maneuver with exuberance. "Me?" she asked, breathlessly. "But last time we were together you couldn't wait to get rid of me."

He pushed her pliable breast against his mouth and nuzzled it. "Last time we were together you had me in such a state that I knew I'd damn well better get rid of you before I did something we'd both regret. I spent the whole long week trying to calm down again, but all I could think of was coming back for more."

A tiny smile twitched at the corners of her mouth and continued throughout her whole body in little waves of delight. Whether or not he realized it, Rusty had just given her a rare and precious gift, the knowledge that he cared enough about her to hurry home to be with her.

She started the massaging movements again. "That's the nicest thing anyone ever said to me. I was afraid you were just sorry for me because I'd been hurt and was all alone."

"In the beginning I was, but then I kissed you that first time, and the jolt I got nearly knocked my socks off."

Again she felt the thrill of conquest. "Really? I thought I was the only one who felt the shock."

He yawned and rubbed his face in the thickness of her sweater. "Sorry," he said, and yawned again. "If you keep rubbing my back and holding me like a baby I'm going to fall asleep."

"That's all right, I don't mind."

He pulled away from her and sat up. "In that case..." he said, and pitched the pillow behind him to land beside the matching pillow at the opposite end of the sofa, "you might as well spend the night."

He reached up and turned off the ceramic lamp on the table, then twisted around to lie down with his head on the pillows. Annelise was too surprised to react as he pulled her down beside him and held her close. "Now lie still and behave yourself, and I promise not to make a pass."

Some imp in her must have spoken as she snuggled against him and muttered, "Oh, darn!"

He swatted her lightly on her conveniently placed bottom. "Watch your mouth, young lady," he growled. "One more crack like that and your virginity is going to be a thing of the past."

She bit back the teasing retort that came to mind, because she knew that if he touched her with passion she wouldn't stop him. Instead she put her arm across his waist and kissed the side of his neck. "Good night, sweet prince," she murmured, quoting from *Hamlet*.

"And flights of angels sing thee to thy rest," Rusty answered, finishing the quote and relaxing instantly into sleep.

Annelise's eyes blinked open. *Where on earth did Rusty learn Shakespeare?*

Annelise struggled out of the depths of slumber, aware that there was something heavy lying across her rib cage and interfering with her breathing. She reached down and her hand touched a large flannel-covered arm.

Rusty! She opened her eyes and got her first glimpse of his living room in the daylight. They were lying on their sides on the huge sofa with his body curled around hers, her bottom fitted into the curve of his groin and his hand cupping her breast.

After her first startled reaction she relaxed and settled into the warmth of his unconscious embrace. A glance at her watch told her that it was a little after eight o'clock, and she blinked. They'd slept for at least nine hours! It had been the deepest, most satisfying sleep she'd ever had. She felt so relaxed and safe wrapped in his arms and cuddled against him.

However, that was bound to change if he woke and found her there. She'd never slept with a man before, but she'd heard that they were usually... uh...aroused...on first waking. Unless she was willing to fulfill the promise her presence in his arms implied she'd better get up—now.

For a moment she was unwilling to move. The thought of making love with Rusty was an enticing one. She wanted to turn over and kiss him awake, feel his arms tighten around her and his mouth ravage hers as it had at the dance, feel the stirring of his maleness as his body quickened with desire.

If he'd pressed the issue last night she would have surrendered to him and gladly, but in the cold light of day she could see the pitfalls, and they were frightening. For Rusty it would be simply release from passion that had built to uncomfortable proportions. It would be that for her, too, but so much more. If she gave herself to him she'd belong to him totally and forever. She didn't want that sort of commitment to any man, and especially not to Rusty Watt. She could easily fall in love with him, and the idea terrified her. Besides, he'd made it plain that he didn't intend to marry in the foreseeable future, and if he did it wouldn't be to the likes of her.

Carefully she moved his arm and slid off the couch. He grunted and moved to a more comfortable position but didn't wake up. Annelise leaned down and kissed him lightly on his battered jaw, then went in search of the bathroom.

The house was an old one, probably built in the twenties, with the living and dining rooms at the front and a hallway off the dining room that led to two bedrooms on her left, the kitchen on her right and the bathroom at the end. It was small but compact and surprisingly neat for a bachelor living alone.

The bathroom was square with the same hardwood floor as the rest of the house and old-fashioned white fixtures, although a shower had been installed above the deep, claw-footed tub. She was using the mouthwash she'd found in the medicine cabinet when the phone rang. Her natural reaction was to answer it, but she immediately realized that wouldn't be too smart. No one would be calling for her here, and it would alert whoever was on the line that Rusty had more than likely entertained an overnight lady friend.

The ringing continued, and after a few seconds she heard Rusty's heavy footsteps come into the hall but turn off at the first bedroom. She could hear his voice but not what he was saying until she opened the door and started back down the hall.

"...should have called you, but I was so beat I came home and sacked out instead," he said, then paused.

"No, I just woke up. I was still asleep when the phone rang.... No! Don't come over, Maybelle, I have to shower and shave and run some errands.... Lunch? Sure. Noon's fine.... Yeah, I missed you too. Bye."

Annelise was standing in the doorway feeling disillusioned and more than a little soiled when he turned around and saw her there. She'd forgotten about Maybelle Holden!

Rusty grinned sheepishly. "Sorry, honey. She called to see if I was home yet."

Annelise nodded. "I heard." Her voice was flat. "Is she your steady girl? Are you engaged?"

His grin disappeared. "No, to both questions. We go out together, mostly to dance. She's a great partner, but I told you, I don't make commitments with women."

He was probably telling the truth, but that didn't mean they weren't lovers. "I also heard you tell her you'd missed her. As I remember, that's the line you handed me last night. How many other women do you intend to sweet-talk with it?"

"Annelise!" Rusty was across the room in one long stride and caught her by the upper arms. "You know better than that. My restraint last night should tell you something about my honorable intentions toward you. Maybelle said she missed me, and I gave the polite response and said I missed her, too. I couldn't very well tell her I'd forgotten she existed because I was going crazy thinking about you."

Some of Annelise's despair faded, and she relaxed under his hold. He was right, she did know better. She may not have been acquainted with Rusty for long, but she knew him well enough to be absolutely certain that he was an honorable man.

She let him pull her against him and put his arms around her. "I was incredibly selfish last night," he said, and there was remorse in his tone. "I wanted you with me so bad that I didn't think of the repercussions. If someone had come over early this morning and found you here it would have been all over town before noon. I'd never forgive myself if I muddied up your spotless reputation."

She put her arms around his waist. "Rusty, I'm a big girl, and I make my own decisions. I wouldn't have stayed if I hadn't wanted to. Besides, it was perfectly innocent—all we did was sleep."

"And who's going to believe that?" Rusty growled. "Hell, I can hardly believe it myself. I must be getting old."

She looked up at him and grinned. "If you give me a few minutes I'm pretty sure I can set your mind at ease on that score."

He hugged her close. "That does it," he said, and released her. "You're going home. Why don't you make some coffee while I shower and shave, and then I'll drive you back to your house."

He was right, she did have to leave, but since it was Monday and she didn't have to work, she wished they could spend the day together. Then she remembered that he was having lunch with Maybelle.

"You don't have to drive me," she said, and started toward the living room. "I walked over, I can walk back."

He caught her and spun her around to face him. "Now listen to me and listen good. If you're seen leaving my house now it'll have the same effect as if someone had come and found you here. My truck's in the garage out back. We can drive out the alley without being seen, so promise you'll stay here and wait until I've made myself presentable." He grinned. "If you don't promise, I'll haul you into the bathroom with me and we can shower together."

She beamed with delight at the picture his words formed in her mind, but she spoke sedately. "Well, when you put it that way I suppose I'd better promise."

She headed for the kitchen and the coffeepot.

Later that day heavy gray clouds extinguished the sun, a cold wind swept across the prairie, and the temperature plummeted. Sometime during the night that followed it began to snow, and by morning the landscape was white. It was nine days before Thanksgiving, and the frost was most definitely on the pumpkin.

Annelise was plagued by a familiar feeling of dread as she left bootprints on the snow-covered sidewalk during her short walk to the library. The holidays were usually difficult for the family of an alcoholic, and hers had been no exception. She'd learned to endure the broken promises and lonely vigils, but she'd never come to terms with the humiliation of accepting food baskets and gaily wrapped gifts delivered by well-meaning, prosperous citizens who represented organizations that brought cheer and sustenance to the "poor and downtrodden."

She shuddered as she turned into the walkway leading to the front door of the library. Her father was dead. There would be no more disappointments or charity, but this year, for the first time, she'd be totally alone. So would her mother.

She unlocked the door and stepped into the chilly building. The thermostat was set low when the rooms weren't in use, and she pushed it up to a comfortable temperature.

The thought of her mother, alone and lonely, brought with it a wave of guilt. If it were at all possible she'd go to Kansas City for Thanksgiving, but it would mean taking at least three days off work. She'd been on the job less than a month, and asking for time off so soon was unthinkable. Besides, she had no way to get there. Her car had been totaled, and she hadn't the faintest idea if it was even possible to go from Raindance to Kansas City on a bus.

She sighed as she sat down at her desk and turned on the computer. No, spending Thanksgiving with her mother was out of the question. The best she could do was call and talk to her before sitting down to her own solitary dinner. Maybe she could find a small hen turkey that wouldn't keep her eating leftovers until she was sick of the sight of them.

There was a lot of traffic through the library in spite of the cold and snow that had fallen gently but steadily all day, and by six o'clock Annelise was happy to tidy up and leave. She'd locked the door behind the last browser and gone to the closet to get her quilted parka when she heard a pounding on the same door. Oh darn, she thought, as she struggled into the jacket. Someone was desperate to pick up or return a book. You'd think that with the library open all day they could get here before closing time.

Muttering to herself as she strode across the room, she turned the lock noisily, and Rusty opened the door and stepped inside. "Glad I got here before you left," he said anxiously. "I was tied up on the phone and not watching the time."

He was wearing his sheepskin jacket, and the ever-present Stetson had snow on the brim, but instead of jeans he wore expertly tailored Western-cut gray slacks that fit like they'd been molded to him. She hadn't seen or heard from him since yesterday morning when he'd dropped her in front of her house and driven off to have lunch with Maybelle Holden.

The puff of wind that blew in with him was fresh and cold, and his cheeks and nose were rosy. Annelise had been afraid that he'd left town again, and she was so glad to see him that it was all she could do to keep from throwing her arms around him. Instead she cleared her throat and said, "I was just closing up. Can I help you find what you're looking for?"

He grinned. "I'm looking for you, you little nut. Why else would I break off in the middle of an important business discussion and come running? I came to pick you up."

He never failed to amaze her. "But Rusty, I only live a block up the street!"

"It's cold and it's dark," he said, as if that explained why she couldn't walk a hundred yards. "Come on, I left the motor running in the Bronco."

He took her arm and led her to the vehicle parked at the curb in a No Parking zone. When they were inside he turned to her. "Do you want to go home before I take you out to dinner?"

"Dinner?" She was inordinately pleased.

He nodded. "I'm leaving for Omaha tomorrow to pick up a reefer—a refrigerated unit—of frozen chickens to haul to California and exchange for vegetables to haul back to Chicago. It'll be a while before I get back, and I want to spend some time with you tonight before I leave."

Her pleasure was mixed with disappointment. Didn't he ever stay home? It was a good thing he wasn't interested in marriage. His children wouldn't even know him. Still, it was the first time he'd sought her out to say goodbye before he left. Maybe he was beginning to think of her as something other than a nuisance.

"Why don't we have dinner at my house? I've got steaks and French rolls in the freezer, and potatoes and salad makings in the refrigerator," Annelise suggested.

Rusty's face split into a wide smile as he shifted and pulled away from the curb. "If you're sure you don't mind cooking, you've got a date."

At the house she turned up the heat, then hung their jackets in the coat closet and took the steaks and rolls out of the freezer. "Sorry I don't have any beer," she said, "but there is a bottle of wine on the counter. The television's in the living room if you'd like to watch the news while I freshen up."

In the bedroom Annelise changed out of the heavy slacks she'd worn to work and put on a lavender and gray plaid full skirt and a lavender sweater. She'd bought the outfit at a closing-out sale at one of the dress shops near the campus during her first semester in college, and she'd filled out some since then. The sweater that had been loose four years ago now discreetly hugged her bosom.

After repairing her makeup with a rose shade of lipstick and blusher, she took the pins out of her chignon and let her hair fall loose to the waist. She knew Rusty liked it that way, and on impulse she picked up her brush and headed for the living room.

He was sitting on the blue flowered sofa watching a football game on television, but he stood and turned it off when she came in. She saw the admiration in his eyes as she handed him the brush. "Would you mind brushing my hair in the back? It's difficult for me to reach."

He took it and turned her around, but his hands lingered on her shoulders. "Mind?" he said huskily. "I'd gladly pay for the privilege."

He lifted the long golden strands away from her nape and planted open-mouthed kisses on the sensitive area. She shivered with sensation, but he quickly raised his head and ran the brush down the luxuriant length of her hair. She sighed and relaxed as his long strokes became caresses. They sent little pinpricks of heat up and down her spine. She'd had no idea that the simple act of letting Rusty brush her hair could be so erotic, but then she should have known. Any time he touched her he sent her senses reeling.

For several minutes there was no sound other than the soft whisper of bristles as they were gently guided through thick, shimmering tresses. Finally Annelise managed to pull herself together enough to murmur drowsily, "I'd better start dinner. You're probably hungry."

Rusty tossed the brush to one side and clasped her around the waist, drawing her back against him. "Oh, I'm hungry all right," he answered as he leaned down and nuzzled the side of her neck, and she knew he wasn't talking about food.

His hands crept upward to cup her breasts while his mouth did stunning things to her throat. She leaned her head back against his chest to make the area more accessible, and he groaned. "Annelise, you shouldn't let me do this. Why don't you ever say no to me?"

She put her hands over the backs of his. "I would if you ever did anything I didn't want you to, but you melt all my resistance." He was driving her crazy with the hot little kisses he was raining on her neck, and the restless kneading of his fingers at her breasts.

"And you're fast melting what's left of my limited self-control," he rasped, then straightened up and pushed her firmly away from him. "For God's sake, go broil something besides me." He patted her on the behind and shoved her gently in the direction of the kitchen before he took off down the hall toward the bathroom.

Rusty splashed cold water on his face and the back of his neck. Why in hell didn't he stay away from Ms. Annelise Kelsey? One of these days he was going to touch her and erupt into mind-searing flames, and when the ashes settled he'd find himself tied to a wife who'd married him for his money, his free and easy life-style gone forever.

He knew that if he ever made love to her, took her virginity, he'd tell her the truth about his background and finances and ask her to marry him. Obviously he had an outdated code of honor, but that's the way he'd been raised and he was stuck with it.

He didn't doubt that Annelise would accept his proposal. He'd do just fine as the rich stud she wanted to father her children. He was a little rough around the edges for her taste, but only because he wanted to be. If pressed into it he could be as smooth and sophisticated as she'd always dreamed her husband would be, and he looked good enough in designer clothes to have been offered modeling jobs while he was at Stanford.

He reached blindly for a towel and buried his dripping face in it. If only she wanted him for himself, rough edges, old comfortable clothes, trucker's wages and all. He suspected that he'd be strongly tempted to give up his precious freedom and settle into the yuppie mold he'd bucked so hard against all these years. If she loved him, really loved him as a wife should love a husband, he'd do anything to make her his and keep her.

He moved the towel around to dry the back of his neck. *Rusty, old boy, you're getting soft in the head. You're not ready to settle down yet, and neither is she. You'd be miserable if you got roped into a shotgun wedding, so cool it. Lust is a lousy foundation for a marriage. Eat her meal, tell her goodbye and get the hell out of here.*

He hung up the towel and reached into his back pocket for his comb. From now on he'd keep his hands off her, but damn, it was a real shame things couldn't have been different. She'd have given him beautiful children!

Annelise set the table in the dining room with Nell Summers's china, crystal and silver, although she was sure Rusty would have been just as happy with plastic. She smiled to herself. While she had him at her mercy he was going to get a dose of culture whether he liked it or not. She'd lived with plastic all her life and had just been waiting for an excuse to use her landlord's good dishes.

Transferring a silk flower arrangement from the living room to the dinner table, she reminded herself that someday she'd have fresh flowers in her house all year round, even if she lived in the snowy part of the country.

Rusty came into the kitchen while she was tearing up greens for the salad and insisted on helping, so she let him finish grilling the steaks. He did a very professional job of it, and she told him so after she'd swallowed her first bite. "You didn't strike me as being the type who knew how to cook," she added.

"I live alone," he reminded her, "and I get a belly-ful of greasy-spoon meals on the road. When I'm home I like home-cooked food. The easiest way to get it is to fix it myself." He glanced at her filled wine glass. "I thought you said you didn't drink."

She chuckled. "I don't. That's ice water, but I tell myself it's white wine, or maybe champagne. There's red wine in your glass, though, not grape juice."

He picked up the glass and took a sip. "Mmm, you must have bought this at Dalrymple's Market. He's the only one in town who sells French wines."

Annelise's eyes widened. "How did you know it was French wine? I thought you only drank beer."

Rusty actually looked disconcerted for a moment before he replied. "I prefer beer, but I'm not unfamiliar with the grape. By the way, did you know there are nonalcoholic wines on the market now? You might prefer them to ice water. I'll bring a bottle next time I see you."

An hour later, after they'd finished eating and had washed and dried the dishes, Annelise made coffee and spooned rich, creamy chocolate ice cream into crystal dessert stemware. Rusty watched with dismay. "Honey, I'm a big man. That little bitty helping isn't going to make a dent in my sweet tooth. Why don't you put mine in a cereal bowl?"

She sighed with frustration. "Just humor me, okay? The crystal is so pretty. I'll refill it as often as you want."

He looked at her with understanding. "Sure, but could I have some chocolate syrup on it?"

They took their dessert and coffee into the living room and sat down together on the sofa. Annelise leaned back and relaxed against the cushions. Rusty put his hand on her knee, but quickly withdrew it. "Hard day?" he asked.

"Busy," she replied. "It usually is on Tuesdays after the library's been closed for a couple of days. The history teacher at the high school has the students studying the French Revolution, and he's divided them into groups and gives each group a different topic for homework. They have to have it completed and turned in before school lets out for the Thanksgiving holiday. As you can imagine they came in disgruntled and griping, so I've been trying to make their task as easy as possible." She grinned. "Boy, could I use a trained research assistant!"

Rusty set his empty ice cream dish on the colonial-style pine coffee table and picked up his cup. "Darn, I'd forgotten that Thanksgiving is coming up so soon. I'll have to make sure to be back by then. Mom would never forgive me if I missed dinner with the rest of the gang."

Again Annelise felt the nagging sense of loneliness. "It must be nice to have a large family to get together with. How many of you are there?"

"Yes, it is," he acknowledged, "but I'm not sure how many we have now. With aunts, uncles and cousins from other parts of the state I'd guess there are twenty or so who can be counted on to come."

He turned to look at her, and his voice softened. "Are you going back to Kansas City to be with your mother?"

She shook her head. "There's no way I can. I don't have transportation, and even if I did I couldn't ask for time off when I've just started to work."

Rusty frowned. "Can't she come here?"

"She doesn't have a car, either, and I'd never be able to convince her to figure out bus schedules. I'll definitely make an effort to get back for Christmas, though.'' She knew she sounded forlorn, but her tone reflected her mood.

He put down his cup. ''Annelise, I have a little money put away. I'd be happy to loan it to you so you could buy another car. It's getting too cold for you to walk every place you go, and it's not safe after dark.''

His generosity touched her to the core of her being, and she swallowed back a lump that threatened to become tears as she sat up and put her untouched ice cream beside his empty dishes. ''That's sweet of you, Rusty, and I appreciate it more than you can possibly know, but I can't let you do that. I'm sure you have other uses for your savings with Christmas coming up and all. Besides, walking is good for me, and Lance takes me grocery shopping....''

Rusty swore. ''I don't want you to have to rely on Lance Farr for anything, and believe me, I can afford to buy you a car—''

Annelise put her fingers to his mouth to silence him. ''But I can't afford to accept it. You see, my mother is going to school to train as a medical assistant. She'll get a small stipend but not enough to live on, so I'm going to send her money every month so she won't have to work. It's a difficult course and she'll need her time to study. I can't make payments on a loan, too.''

Rusty put his hand up and stroked her face. ''Honey, listen to me. I have money I don't need sitting in the bank, and it worries me to have you trying to get by without a car. I don't care when, or even if, you pay me back. You can think of it as an investment in my own peace of mind.''

Again she blinked back tears of gratitude and appreciation. Nobody had ever offered to lend her money before. When she'd bought the Plymouth no bank would touch the loan, and she'd been forced to deal with a loan shark who'd charged her an outrageous amount of interest. Rusty's faith in her was worth more than any amount of money.

She turned her head and kissed the palm that was cupping her cheek. "I know you're generous to a fault when it comes to helping people, but you've already done far more for me than I can ever repay." Her voice quivered with emotion. "I can't let you tie up your hard-earned savings on the chance that I'd start paying you back eventually, but I love you with all my heart for offering."

The groan that seemed torn from him was one of true anguish as he lowered his head and captured her trembling mouth with his own.

Chapter Seven

Without breaking off the kiss Rusty lifted Annelise and set her on his lap as he silently cursed himself for losing control of the situation. He was only human, for God's sake, and she was so sweet, and so responsive, and so incredibly loving that he would have had to be a saint to resist her.

Her breast exactly fit his large hand, and it was soft but high and firm. His fingers probed and stroked and ached to tear away the layers of clothing and feel the warm, smooth, bare skin and the rough, pebbly texture of her nipple.

Her lips parted slightly, and he rubbed them with the tip of his tongue, encouraging her to allow him full entry. *Careful,* he told himself as desire raged through him, *don't be greedy. Teach her, don't scare her away.*

Annelise's mouth relaxed and opened further, and Rusty's tongue encountered her white, even teeth. She tasted clean and fresh with just a hint of the tangy dressing from the tossed salad. He forced himself to be content to explore her teeth and the underside of her lips, and reveled in her arms holding him and her fingers caressing the back of his head.

For a woman of twenty-two she was incredibly inexperienced. That drunken father of hers must have really turned her off men. She didn't even know about open-mouth kisses. The thought pleased him, and he managed to get a grip on his shattered control and break it off, although his lips still rested at the corner of her mouth. He was no despoiler of virgins, but surely there was no harm in teaching her the preliminaries of love-making.

The small part of his mind that was still functioning rationally screamed warnings, but he was in no condition to heed them.

Even as she breathed in much-needed air, Annelise sought and found Rusty's lips again. Before she'd met him she'd had no idea that a simple thing like a kiss could shake up the whole nervous system. She throbbed in the most embarrassing places, and her body clamored for more, much more.

Their mouths clung, but this time he put his thumb on her chin and pinched gently, causing her mouth to open. She gasped as his tongue thrust between her teeth and dueled with hers. Her first reaction was to reject the intimate invasion, but he was being so tender, so careful not to startle her further as he explored the inside of her mouth and gentled her own defensive tongue until it began to stroke his in return.

When he finally withdrew she felt empty, and she realized that her fingers were digging into the hard flesh and muscles of his shoulders while her breasts flattened against his chest as she struggled to get even closer. Her breathing was labored, but no more so than his, and she could feel his heart pounding as savagely as hers.

She buried her face in his shoulder until she was reasonably sure she could breathe and talk all at the same time. Then she leaned back and nuzzled the pulse that throbbed under his jaw. "I—I've never been kissed like that before," she whispered breathlessly.

His hand roamed over her back. "I know. Did you like it?" He seemed to be having trouble with his voice, also.

"Oh, my, yes, but I don't know what you wanted of me. How can I make it good for you, too?"

His hand found its way under her sweater and moved over her satin slip. "You were doing fine," he murmured, and nibbled at her earlobe. "Don't you feel my heart hammering? Just do what comes naturally. It gets easier with practice."

She ran a finger over the jaw she'd been nuzzling. "Do...do you suppose we could try it again? Practice, I mean."

He chuckled. "Of course. We'll keep at it until you get it right, but first—" he slid the bolo tie over his head and dropped it on the couch beside him "—unbutton my shirt."

He put his hand back under her sweater, and hesitantly she reached up and began working on the small pearl buttons. "Are you too warm?" she asked.

"Much too warm," he replied. She heard the amusement in his tone, and blushed at her own naiveté.

Annelise's fingers trembled as she struggled with the tiny fastenings. Each one that opened revealed another few inches of dark reddish-brown hair covering an immense chest that positively rippled with muscles. When she got to the waistband of his slacks she stopped, then jerked her hand away when she realized where the heel of it was resting.

She knew her face was flaming with embarrassment, but Rusty quietly picked up her hand, kissed the palm and put it on his bare chest. The hair was thick and soft, and it curled around her fingers, making her tingle with the most incredible feeling.

"Would you like to take off your sweater?" he asked.

He was already stroking her under the garment, and the idea of removing it was exciting, but she paused. "Do you think it would be all right?" she asked timidly. "I'm not in the habit of taking off my clothes on a date."

"I won't ask you to do anything you don't want to do, honey, but I'd like to see you without it."

Thoughtfully she wove her fingers through the hair on his chest without looking at him directly before she finally said, "All right," and raised both her arms.

He slid the sweater over her head and laid it across the back of the couch without taking his gaze from her. "You have skin like satin," he murmured, and rubbed the palms of his hands over her bare shoulders and upper arms. "It's the color of a peach milkshake, and it shimmers in the light."

He drew her to him and settled her against his furry chest, then bent his head and traced kisses across her creamy flesh. "Oh, yes," he breathed, "that's much better."

She couldn't agree more, and she clutched a fistful of the short hair over his rib cage as ripples of pleasure started deep within her and spread throughout her body.

Feverishly anxious to give him the same pleasure, she rubbed her cheek against him and fastened her open mouth over his large, flat nipple. It had a thick, slightly rough texture, and she ran her tongue around its perimeter, then drew on it more fully with little sucking movements.

His whole body tensed, and she immediately stopped. "I'm sorry," she said anxiously, and sat up, "I didn't mean to hurt you."

He cupped her face with his hands and kissed her, a deep, passionate, hungry kiss. "You didn't hurt me," he assured her in a voice that grated with frustration. "I just wasn't expecting you to do that. It had approximately the effect of sticking my finger in a light socket."

"Is that good or bad?" she asked in a bewildered tone.

He kissed each of her eyelids. "My little sweetheart, how could it be anything but good with you?" he murmured. "If you want the truth you're about to blow my fuses. Now let's practice that kiss once more, and then I'm getting out of here while I still can."

He put his arms around her and cuddled her close. "Open your mouth," he whispered, and she complied as he covered it with his own and taught her well.

For the first time since he'd owned it, Rusty ground the gears on his truck tractor as he backed out of the garage and shifted into low. He swore lustily. He'd probably wreck the transmission just as he'd already ruined any chance of a night's sleep.

He maneuvered the tractor into the street and headed it toward the highway. It hadn't been his intention to leave town until early the next morning, but after an hour of making out with Annelise Kelsey he was too steamed up to sleep, so he decided to spend the night on the road. By the time he reached Omaha maybe he'd be calmed down enough to catch a snooze before he picked up the reefer.

At the highway he turned east and settled comfortably in the seat. There was practically no traffic on this road at night, and he'd driven it so many times that it was almost like being on automatic pilot.

He wanted a cigarette. Even though it had been more than two years since he'd quit smoking he still sometimes caught himself reaching into his shirt pocket for the nonexistent package, usually during times of stress or boredom. Well, he sure hadn't been bored this evening, so it must be stress. God knows, Annelise inspired enough of that in him to set up all kinds of cravings.

He shifted uncomfortably. He was too old for this sort of nonsense. If he wanted a woman he knew several who would be happy to accommodate him, so why did he keep coming back to the one he couldn't have?

He frowned. No, that wasn't entirely accurate. He could have had Annelise. If he'd picked her up and carried her to her bedroom she wouldn't have refused him. Hell, he'd had her so aroused that she'd have responded eagerly and begged him to teach her how to please him even more.

His hands clasped the steering wheel so tightly that his knuckles were white, and in spite of the cold night air he was sweating. *Nice going, buddy,* he told himself sarcastically. *If you keep up that train of thought, nothing short of walking to Omaha will cool you down.*

As usual, Annelise heard nothing from Rusty while he was gone. He'd walked away from her after those passionate kisses Tuesday night and disappeared. She hadn't slept worth a darn since.

Was he having the same problem? Probably not. No doubt he had women all over the country who took care of his physical needs during his long trips. After all, he was a bachelor, and so totally *male*.

A stab of painful jealousy brought with it a comforting doubt. She had good reason to know that he was a passionate man, but she couldn't believe that he was an indiscriminate lover. If he had been he would have seduced her by now. Twice he'd had her in vulnerable situations when she would have done anything he wanted, but he hadn't acted on his advantage. Not that he'd been unaffected. Both times he'd made no secret of his arousal, but he'd controlled his desire and walked away. Her good sense told her she should be grateful. She didn't want to get emotionally involved with any man, but especially not with Rusty. She should be the one who walked away instead of aching for more.

Now it was Sunday, and as she came out of church into the glare of sunlight on the snow she was met by Mayor and Mrs. Farr and Lance. "Annelise," Margaret Farr said, "how pretty you look. Is that a new coat? It's such a rich shade of brown."

Annelise smiled at the compliment. "Thank you, Margaret, and yes, it is new. I got it at Harcourt's pre-Thanksgiving sale. My old one saw me all the way through college and was getting pretty shabby." She turned her head to include Jim and Lance in her smile.

"It's Thanksgiving we wanted to talk to you about," Margaret said. "We'd like you to have dinner with us if you're going to be in town."

Annelise's smile widened. "Why, thank you. I'd love to. I've sort of dreaded spending the day alone."

Lance spoke up. "I have tickets for the annual high-school football game between our Prairie Pups and Webster's Beavers. They're playing on our field this year. Would you like to go with me? The parade starts at noon and the game at one. It will fill up the time until dinner at five."

Webster was another small town west of Raindance, and there was apparently a legendary rivalry between the two schools. "Sounds like fun," Annelise said. "That is, unless there's something I can do to help with the meal preparations." She looked questioningly at Margaret.

"Not a thing," the other woman said. "My sister and her husband and two grown daughters will be coming for dinner, too, so I'll have plenty of assistance."

The snow was all gone by Thanksgiving, and the day dawned sunny and warmer than usual. Even the persistent wind had calmed to a light breeze as Annelise dressed in jeans, a sweatshirt and thick woolen socks with her Reeboks. Warm for the Nebraska prairie in late November was still not much above freezing, and no one would plan to stand around all afternoon outside without wearing heavy clothing.

Lance parked his car in front of her house, and she donned her quilted parka and gloves before they left to walk the two blocks to the business district to watch the parade. He was also dressed in jeans with a heavy leather jacket and a woolen cap pulled over his thinning hair.

Annelise was used to huge, professionally choreographed parades that extended for many blocks and featured numerous bands, massive floats, magnificent show horses and celebrities riding on the backs of flashy

convertibles and waving at the crowds. She tried not to
let her surprise and disappointment show as she beheld
the Raindance version.

It was all of two blocks long and featured the high-
school band, the football team and cheering section,
several homemade floats on wagons, the boy and girl
scouts and Mayor Farr and the high-school principal in
an open classic convertible that Lance informed her had
been borrowed from Ernie Stone, a local mechanic who
bought broken-down cars and fixed them up.

The parade had formed at the school and marched
the three blocks west to Main Street, then turned north
and continued to the highway where it disbanded as
everyone went their separate ways. Annelise glanced at
Lance, to find him watching her with laughter in his
eyes. "Well, what did you expect?" he joked. "Ticker
tape and the Marine band?"

Annelise laughed with him. "Yeah, I guess I did.
Silly, but when anyone mentions 'parade,' I think big.
They didn't even have a clown!"

Rather than fight for a place to park near the football field, they decided to walk to the school complex,
which consisted of an elementary school, a junior high
and high school and a separate building that housed the
auditorium-gym, showers, dressing rooms and band
practice quarters. A playground was situated to one side
of the elementary building, and behind that was the
football stadium.

Annelise had been past the school buildings but
hadn't paid much attention, so she was surprised to see
that the "stadium" was an open field with goal posts at
each end and chalked yardage markers in between. A
short chain link fence separated the players from the
spectators, and crude wooden bleachers had been

erected at the fifty-yard line along one side, the center of which was reserved for the red-and-white-clad student cheering section.

By the time they got there the extra seats were all taken, and they joined the overflow standing behind the fence. The game was well into the second quarter when, during a time out, Annelise's glance roamed over the spectators, and she spotted Rusty standing on the other side of the bleachers.

He was looking right at her and glaring, and she had the sinking feeling that he wasn't pleased to see her. She smiled and waved, but he merely nodded and turned away.

Now what had she done? Surely he didn't still disapprove of her friendship with Lance. She'd told him that she wasn't trying to seduce the mayor's son into marriage. Besides, what right did Rusty Watt have to approve or disapprove? If he'd invited her to spend Thanksgiving with him and his family she'd have been delighted to accept, but he hadn't even bothered to contact her when he got home. Damn him! Hadn't their passionate goodbye meant anything to him?

Annelise told herself she wasn't going to look his way again, but it was no use. Her head kept turning and her eyes kept focusing on the big, lovable, country-boy type of man who managed to keep her in a constant state of turmoil without even trying. She was never sure whether he'd hug and kiss her or rip her apart with sharp-edged words whenever they met.

Soon she realized that he wasn't alone. There were two other men with him, both big, brawny and dressed like Rusty in jeans, sheepskin jackets and cowboy hats. The three of them cheered and jeered as the Prairie Pups alternately scored and fumbled until the score was six to seven in favor of the Beavers. Then, with twenty seconds showing on the clock, the quarterback dropped back and launched a spiral over the outstretched hands of the defender and into the arms of his tight end for a touchdown!

The crowd went wild, and Annelise and Lance threw their arms around each other and hugged. They were still embracing as they watched while the kick went squarely through the uprights and the whistle blew, setting the spectators off again with enthusiastic screams of joy as the scoreboard changed to show thirteen to seven at the half in favor of the home team.

Again they hugged, and Lance's cheek was cold as it pressed against Annelise's equally chilly one. The hood that was attached to her parka had slid back revealing her yellow hair piled on top of her head in a loose knot and held in place with combs and invisible hairpins.

A voice as cold as Lance's cheek sent icy splinters down her spine. "Is something going on here I should know about? After all, Annelise is my foundling. I feel a certain responsibility for her."

They quickly broke apart and turned to face Rusty, whose furious expression was like that of a father who has found his teenage daughter in bed with the town bounder. Lance, who either didn't notice or chose not to acknowledge Rusty's sarcasm, looked at him and said, "Hello, Rusty. Exciting game, huh?"

Rusty tipped his Stetson back with one finger. "I can see how it would be for you. When are you going back to Harvard, Lance?"

Lance looked surprised by the question. "Uh, next semester." His gaze strayed to the two men who had just joined Rusty. "Oh, hi, Bud, Jack. You guys enjoying the game?"

The shorter of the two spoke. "Hey, that was some play, wasn't it? I hear that Yarborough kid has had offers from several universities already."

Rusty had pinned Annelise with his smoldering glance, and it was all she could do to keep from shrinking back guiltily, even though she didn't have anything to be guilty about.

"Annelise," he said, breaking into the conversation of the other two men. "I'd like you to meet my brothers, Bud—" he nodded toward the one who had been talking to Lance "—and Jack." All three Watts were over six feet, but Rusty was the biggest. "Guys, Lance's little gal here is Annelise Kelsey, Raindance's new librarian."

Lance's little gal, indeed. She knew he was goading her, and she'd have liked nothing better than to tell him what she thought of his chauvinistic behavior, but she wasn't going to give him the satisfaction of seeing her lose her temper in front of members of his family. It hadn't escaped her notice that this was the first time he'd introduced her to any of them.

She put out her hand to Bud. "How do you do, Bud," she said with all the dignity at her command as he clasped it. Then she offered it to the other one. "And Jack," she said sweetly. "I'm so pleased to finally meet some of Rusty's family." She managed to sound just a tiny bit hurt by the previous omission, and was chagrined to realize that she really was.

"So you're the youngster Rusty collided with a while back," Jack exclaimed as recognition dawned. He squeezed her hand and grinned at Rusty. "Hey, little brother, I hate to tell you this, but she's no kid. She's all grown up, and frankly, it worries me that you didn't notice."

He winked playfully at Annelise, and they all laughed except Rusty, who muttered something unprintable under his breath. "I noticed," he growled, "but I'm not her type. Ms. Kelsey is one of those liberated ladies who doesn't need a man to be happy. She can take care of herself, can't you, honey?" The "honey" wasn't spoken as an endearment.

"I certainly hope so," Annelise said quietly. Her anger was gone, and the pain he'd inflicted sounded in her voice. "You see, I've never yet met a man I could trust not to let me down. Now, if you'll excuse us—" she turned to Lance and reached out for him "—we'd better get over to the snack stand before the hot coffee's all gone."

Lance gazed at her troubled expression and put his arm around her waist. "Nice to see you fellows," he called over his shoulder as they headed for the PTA-sponsored food sale. "Enjoy the rest of the game."

Annelise waited off to the side as Lance bought big cups of steaming coffee. "Come on," he said as he handed one to her. "I know a place where we can sit down and talk."

She kept her gaze straight ahead and didn't look back to see if Rusty and his brothers were still around as Lance led her across the playground and around to the front of the high school. There they sat on a bench that was built into a recess in the building out of the path of the cold breeze and took sips of their coffee.

Lance was the first to speak. "Annelise, is there something going on between you and Rusty Watt?"

She slowly shook her head. "No, not really. He feels responsible for me because of the accident. We're attracted to each other and have shared a few kisses, but we really don't have anything in common. I—I made the mistake of telling him that when I married, I would put financial security and prestige before passionate love, so now he thinks I've decided you'd be the ideal husband and that I'm trying to seduce you.''

"Are you?" he asked quietly.

"Oh, Lance," she turned to look into his gray eyes beneath the dark-framed glasses, "you know better than that. Such a thing never even occurred to me until he accused me of it. I told him we were just good friends, but I guess when he saw us together today he jumped to all the wrong conclusions again. He says he won't let me trap you into a loveless marriage.''

Lance snorted. "That's damn big of him considering I never asked for or wanted his protection. You can tell him for me that I'm perfectly capable of deciding whether I want to be seduced or not, and to kindly step out of the way and let you have at me.''

Startled, Annelise looked up only to see the corners of his mouth twitch with the effort to suppress a grin. She giggled, and then they laughed together. "Shame on you," she said, still shaking with mirth, "you're not taking this seriously.''

"Are you?" He was no longer laughing.

She turned her hands palm up in a gesture of helplessness. "Yes, I guess I am. I don't like him to think badly of me.''

"Are you in love with him?"

For a moment she didn't answer. "No," she said finally. "At least I hope not. I have no faith in love. It's a trap to get a woman to live in bondage with some man. I don't want any part of it.''

"That bad, huh?" he mused. "Tell me about it."

Although she'd never before discussed her background with anybody but Rusty and Dr. Cole, she

somehow knew she could trust Lance, and she told him
everything. It was easier this time, and in the telling she
was better able to understand some of her parents' mistakes.

"...I made up my mind a long time ago that I'd never
marry and chance going through what my mother did,"
she said in conclusion, "but now I know I'd like to have
children. I'm not the type to be an unwed mother, so I'll
be extremely selective about the man I pick for their father."

The Prairie Pups won by a score of twenty to fourteen in a hard-fought and suspenseful game, but Rusty
sat silently in Bud's new pickup while his brothers re-
hashed the finer points on their ride back to the ranch.
He'd made a jackass of himself again, and he felt like
the bastard Annelise no doubt thought he was.

Why did he fly off the handle every time he saw her
with Lance Farr? If she wanted the rich little egghead
for her husband of convenience what business was it of
his, anyway? Rusty knew his original excuse that she
wouldn't make Lance happy was ludicrous. All the
money in the world couldn't buy the erotic bliss she'd
give her husband freely and without restraint.

He muttered a short, succinct oath, loud and coarse,
before he remembered he wasn't alone. It immediately
captured the attention of both his brothers. "What's the
matter?" asked Jack. "You don't agree that it was a
brilliant pass?"

Rusty brought his thoughts up short and knew he
looked as sheepish as he felt. "Sorry, I was thinking of
something else."

Both men laughed. "Obviously," said Bud. "So
who's the woman who's got you so frustrated you can't

even enjoy a dynamite football game?'' A look of surprise crossed Bud's ragged face, and then he answered his own question. ''Jeez, it's that girl with the Farr kid, isn't it? The one involved in the accident.''

''Oh, knock it off,'' Rusty grated, furious with himself for not being more cautious.

The two brothers were instantly serious, and it was Jack who spoke next. ''She's not exactly your style, pal. I know I teased you about not noticing that she's all grown up. I was obviously wrong, but she's still pretty young, and a *librarian*. Besides, she looks like the champagne and hors d'oeuvres type. You sure you know what you're getting yourself into?''

Champagne and hors d'oeuvres type was Watt family slang for a very classy lady.

Rusty glared. ''I'm not 'getting myself into' anything. I just feel responsible for her because of the accident.''

Jack raised one eyebrow. ''Hey, it's us, big brothers Jack and Bud. We may look and act like we've never been off the farm, but we all minored in psychology at Stanford, remember? Don't sling that old stuff my way. I know you're hurtin', so tell us about it.''

Rusty sighed. Jack was right. All three brothers had studied psychology at Stanford, but Jack was the one who should have made a career of it. He had a way of relating to people that made them open up to him, and he'd been most successful in helping friends and family members with their more difficult problems.

''Sorry,'' Rusty said, ''I didn't mean to snap at you, but there really isn't anything to tell. I admit she gets under my skin, but I don't intend to do anything about it. You're right, she's a classy lady and I'm a good ol' boy from down on the farm. We have absolutely nothing in common, and she's too young to interest me as anything but a novelty that I'm smart enough not to toy with.''

Both brothers looked skeptical. "Why haven't you brought her out to the ranch to meet your family?" Bud asked. "See how she reacts to you on your own turf?"

Rusty shook his head. "I can't. When I found out she was going to be alone for Thanksgiving I was sorely tempted to invite her to spend it with us, but she thinks you all just work on the ranch. She doesn't know that we own it. She also doesn't know that I have anything more than a high-school education, and that's the way I want it. I can't take her home—someone's bound to let the truth slip out."

"Good Lord, man!" Bud shouted. "How can you expect her to be the kind of woman you want if you don't give her a chance to know who you are?"

"But that's just it," Rusty explained. "I *am* the Rusty Watt she knows: truck driver, beer guzzler and small-town hick. That's what I'll always be no matter how rich I am or how much education I've got. I'm not going to change, and neither is she. We were both born with our tastes and preferences, and we'll die with them. Neither of us could be happy living the life of the other."

Bud was silenced, so it was Jack who spoke. "In that case, Russ, you better make damn sure you don't get any more involved with her than you apparently already are."

Rusty pulled his hat down to shade his eyes and crossed his arms over his chest. "I don't intend to," he said emphatically.

Chapter Eight

The library was open as usual on the Friday after Thanksgiving, but it was a slow day and Annelise spent most of it sitting behind the desk with too much time to think.

Except for the hurtful run-in with Rusty, Thanksgiving day had been a pleasant one, and even that unfortunate incident had served a purpose. Telling her story to Lance had helped her to put her unhappy past into better perspective, and for the first time she was a little unsure of the soundness of her bias against love and marriage.

Maybe it did work for some people. It certainly appeared to have for Lance's parents. Jim and Margaret Farr had been married for almost thirty years, and they still called each other "sweetheart" and "darling" and radiated a closeness that couldn't be an act.

Even though Lance was an only child, yesterday the big house had been filled with aunts, uncles, cousins and, a special treat for Annelise since she'd never known her own, his eighty-four-year-old grandmother. They were a close-knit, loving family and had made her feel welcome.

It wasn't until Lance had taken her back to her own empty and lonely dwelling that her thoughts returned to her troubled relationship with Rusty. What did he want from her? More important, what did she want from him? She was going to have to resolve this, and soon if she expected to escape heart-whole.

A ripple of foreboding ran through her. It might already be too late.

Promptly at six o'clock Annelise stepped out of the library door and locked it behind her. A cold blast of night air whipped around her, and she shivered as it cut right through her woolen slacks and even managed to invade her heavy jacket. The weather report had been for snow, and the first tiny shards of sleet stung her exposed cheeks as she hurried down the walkway to the sidewalk.

It was only then that she saw Rusty's Bronco parked at the curb, and Rusty standing beside it.

He opened the door and stepped forward to take her arm. "Come and get inside," he said without bothering to say hello or ask if she wanted a ride.

Annelise wasn't angry enough with him to insist on walking, but neither was she willing to thank him for coming to save her from the weather. She settled herself on the passenger seat while Rusty climbed in on the other side and pulled away from the curb.

The heater was running and it was warm and cozy in the four-wheel-drive vehicle. Neither of them spoke as he circled the two blocks to end up facing south, and parked in front of her house. Clutching her purse, she opened the door. "Thanks for the ride," she said, and jumped out, shutting the door behind her.

Without looking back she heard Rusty get out and knew he wasn't going to let her get away with her evasive ploy. He was right behind her as she entered the house.

She walked into the living room and turned on the light before facing him. He didn't look angry as she'd feared he would. Instead he watched her with a brooding intensity that threw her into a state of confusion. Now what?

She took a deep breath. "Thank you for being so thoughtful as to come and get me," she said uncertainly, "but I really don't think we have anything to say to each other, so—"

"I have something to say to you," he interrupted quietly but firmly as he unbuttoned his heavy jacket and took it off, then hung it over the back of a nearby chair. "I want to apologize for my behavior yesterday. I know I made a fool of myself, and I'm sorry if I embarrassed you." He removed his Stetson and held it.

Darn! Why did he always do this to her? She'd managed to convince herself that she and Rusty had no basis for any kind of relationship, and now here he was standing before her, hat in hand, looking like a giant teddy bear begging to be stroked.

She felt her resistance melting and slipped out of her own jacket, hoping the activity would shore it up. "That's a nice apology," she acknowledged, and was pleased that her tone didn't betray her wavering composure, "but it doesn't excuse the way you keep jumping to unlikely conclusions and making unjustified accusations."

"I know," he said, and rolled the brim of the hat that he held with both hands.

Her jacket slid to the floor unnoticed as she tried once more to bolster her indignation. "It's none of your business if I go out with Lance or any other man."

His gaze lowered to the hat brim he was twisting. "I know," he said again.

She clenched her teeth. She was beginning to feel like a mother scolding a repentant son. "You knew I was going to be alone on Thanksgiving, but you didn't invite me to spend it with you—"

"I couldn't," he interrupted but offered no further explanation.

"I didn't expect you to," she hurriedly assured him, "but you have no right to be upset because Lance Farr and his family did. You didn't even let me know you were back in town. You blow hot and cold, and I don't have to put up with your temper tantrums."

He still didn't look up. "I know you don't."

Finally her composure snapped. "Damn it, Rusty," she shouted and waved her arms, "why don't you argue with me, defend yourself?"

He raised his head then, and she saw the anguish in his expressive eyes. "Because everything you've said is the truth. I have no argument or defense. I deserve anything you want to say to me." He tossed the battered hat onto a nearby chair. "The problem is that I've never been tortured by jealousy before, and I don't know how to control it."

She blinked. "Jealousy?"

He reached out and ran his finger down her cheek. "We've had this conversation before, remember? You were surprised then, too. Why do you find it difficult to believe that it tears me apart to find you in the arms of another man?''

"But I wasn't—"

His finger continued its journey along her jaw. "Yes you were, and when I saw you and Lance together like that something snapped. It took all the willpower I could muster to keep from grabbing you away from him and dragging you off to my cave like a damned Neanderthal.''

She opened her mouth to protest, but he closed it again with his thumb and finger. "Save your breath; it's the truth. I didn't come out of the red fog until you'd taken all the abuse from me you intended to and walked off. By then the damage was done, and I couldn't even try to repair it until we'd both calmed down."

She licked her dry lips with the tip of her tongue. "Rusty..."

He lifted her chin, then leaned down and touched his mouth to hers, once, then twice, and by the third time she was lost. "Oh, Rusty," she moaned as she swayed toward him, "what am I going to do with you?"

He swept her into his arms and shattered her with the hot, moist kiss she'd been seeking. "Just love me, sweetheart," he said, his voice strained with desire, "and let me love you."

Annelise wasn't sure what his definition of love was, but by then she didn't care. Before Rusty she'd had no experience with the magnetic pull of desire, the intense heat of passion or the throbbing ache of wanting, and she was helpless in the whirlpool of churning, swirling emotions.

He was holding her off the floor, and she twined her arms around his neck and opened her mouth as he'd taught her, before capturing his. He was balanced in a wide-legged stance to absorb her full weight, and one hand moved to her buttocks and pushed her hard against him, letting her feel what she was doing to him.

It was the most intimate embrace she'd ever shared with a man, and her whole body tingled in response. Her tongue enticed his into her eager mouth, and she sucked gently, eliciting a sound like a cry of torment from deep in his throat as his arms tightened to a strangling hold.

When she could no longer breathe she was forced to break off the tempestuous kiss. Unwilling to interrupt the erotic plunder, Rusty muttered, "No" as he brushed his lips across her face in search of the ones she'd just denied him.

She turned her head and murmured, "Darling, I can't catch my breath when you hold me so tightly."

Her gentle protest seemed to snap him back to reality, and he immediately loosened his hold and let her slide slowly and enticingly down his body until her feet touched the floor. She moved her arms to put them around his waist and leaned against him. They were both breathing heavily.

"Annelise," Rusty muttered, his voice ragged, "You should be branded with an *I* for incendiary! One of these times my control is going to go up in flames, and then there'll be hell to pay."

"Would it really be so bad?" she asked timidly, more than a little hurt that he would think so.

"You know it would." He turned her and led her to the sofa.

They sat down, and he pulled the hidden pins from her chignon, releasing her hair to tumble down her back, then took her in his arms and murmured, "Does this mean you accept my apology?'' He still sounded shaken.

She snuggled into his embrace. "Have I ever denied you anything?'' she asked against his plaid wool shirt.

"No.'' He cupped his hand around her breast. "You trust me to apply the brakes, but my brake lining's getting awfully thin, and I'm not sure how much longer I'm going to be able to do that. I came here tonight intending to apologize and then leave.'' He put his hand under her sweater, and his palm was slightly rough against her bare skin.

He sucked in his breath. "You'll notice how I botched that good intention,'' he said wryly. "Raise your arms.''

She did, and he pulled the sweater over her head, leaving her with a filmy pink satin and lace bra as covering.

A small gasp escaped her as she felt the warm flush of embarrassment at being exposed. "Come up here where I can get at you,'' Rusty said, and lifted her onto his lap.

He kissed the soft rise of her breasts, starting up a clamor in the pit of her stomach that spread downward as he released a nipple from its confinement and took it in his mouth.

She clasped his wide shoulders and dug in to keep her balance. His seeking fingers found and loosened the front clip and brushed the material out of the way as his hands took over the support the garment had been constructed to give.

He raised his head to look at her, and his eyes were dark with passion. "I always knew you were beautiful, but I didn't realize you were so nearly perfect. Your breasts are firm and ripe, and nestle in my hands as though they'd been formed to fit. They have the elusive, uncaptured scent of sun and rain and suckling babies.''

He laid his head against her sensitized softness, and she put her arms around him and held him there. She didn't want to interrupt the cherished interlude, but she longed to run her hands over the hair-roughened bareness of his chest again, and to feel it against her own nudity.

His smooth-shaven cheek was warm against her skin, and she stroked the exposed side of his face as she buried her own in the red highlights of his dark brown hair. ''Aren't you going to take your shirt off?'' she asked shyly.

''Do you want me to?'' He sounded pleased.

''Yes, I like to touch you.''

He released her and leaned back. ''I like to have you touch me.'' His tone was husky as he unsnapped the pearl grippers, common fastenings on Western garments.

He tossed the shirt aside giving her a full view of the upper half of his magnificent, muscular torso. She put out her hand and touched him tentatively. The gnarled hair curled around her fingers and she swirled them through the thick mat, then drew circles around first one taut nipple and then the other.

He seemed content to let her explore until her inquiring fingers began to travel downward to his waist and across his flat, hard stomach. She'd almost reached the band of his low-riding jeans when he shuddered and captured her hand. ''That's enough, you little tease.'' He sounded breathless. ''Any lower and we're both going to be in big trouble.'' His hand at her back guided her closer. ''Come here, I want to feel you against me.''

She was both appalled and excited to realize that she really had been teasing him, but he didn't seem to mind as he cradled her to him, her breasts soft against his thoroughly masculine chest. She pressed wet little kisses on his bare skin while he sought and found the fastening on her slacks. He loosened it and slid the zipper part way down so he could caress her lower back and hips.

Annelise's muscles jumped involuntarily. She'd never allowed a man that sort of liberty before, but Rusty's hand came to rest on the curve of her hip bone and went no further. "You have the sexiest little tush that ever wiggled into a tight pair of slacks," he said, and lowered his head to kiss her. "It's exciting just watching you walk."

"Did anyone ever tell you you're a dirty old man?" She giggled with pleasure while he nibbled on her earlobe.

"Yeah," was the only answer she got as his tongue made little flicking forays along her jaw.

When he got to her mouth he took it in a kiss that burned with the repressed desire that consumed them both. His restless hand clenched the flesh of her hip, and she understood that it was only with great effort that he kept it from straying into even more dangerous territory.

Her arms tightened around his neck and she strained to get closer to him until her breasts flattened against his chest, and she could feel his heart racing. Her senses were reeling when he reluctantly released her lips and buried his face in the sweet-scented hollow of her neck.

She was left suspended in a purgatory not of her own choosing, and she uttered a discordant cry of protest as she stiffened against the tempestuous emotions that had been frustrated and denied. "Rusty, please..."

He quickly removed his hand from her warm bare hip and lifted his head. "Annelise, we've got to stop *now*." His tone was gravelly with need. "If we go any further, I won't be able to. My God, sweetheart, I can only stand so much."

The agony in his voice penetrated her fog of torment, and she relaxed and straightened.

His face was as tortured as his voice, and she put her fingers to the mouth that had raised her to heights she hadn't known existed. "Rusty, I knew what we were leading up to, and I didn't want to stop."

He kissed her fingers, then took her hand and held it against his cheek. "I know, neither did I, but it's not fair to either of us to let this relationship continue. It isn't going anywhere and we both know it. That's what I came here tonight to tell you, but then I made the mistake of touching you, and, as usual, I forgot everything but how much I want you, need you."

"But I don't understand...." If he wanted her and she wanted him, why did he stop?

"Yes you do." There was a touch of impatience in his tone. "But I'll spell it out for you anyway. You're not the type for a short fling, and I don't make commitments to women. You want something totally different than what I can give you, and I like my life just the way it is."

Lifting her off his lap he set her on the couch beside him, then stood and crossed the room to pick up his coat. "I'm leaving Monday for a long haul that will keep me on the road for at least a couple of months. That should give me time to work you out of my system."

He put on the jacket and buttoned it. "When I come back I'm not going to get in touch with you. If we meet on the street, as we probably will from time to time, we'll say hello and keep on going."

He picked up his hat and turned to face her as he put it on. "You're sweet, and very dear to me." In spite of himself his voice was filled with tenderness. "But in the realities of life and love you're still a child, and I'm not going to be the one to wake you up and spoil your dreams."

She started to walk toward him, but he held up his hand. "No, if you care about me at all don't come any closer. I've just run out of self-control."

He strode hurriedly across the room and out the door, leaving Annelise standing alone, wide-eyed and stunned.

It was a long night, and although Annelise finally went to bed, what little sleep she got was fitful and marred by vague, uneasy dreams. Actually they were subconscious memories rather than dreams—unhappy memories of her father. But when she finally got up at five-thirty she had no clear picture of them. All that was left was a sluggish, depressed feeling, and a nagging certainty that with Rusty's departure she'd lost something precious, but she didn't know what to do about it.

She turned on the light and went to the kitchen where she made coffee and poured herself a glass of orange juice. Her hand trembled, and some of the juice spilled. The last time she'd been this thoroughly undone was when her father had died.

Her father. Kenneth Kelsey. It was Rusty who'd rejected her, so why was it her father's image that haunted her? She was going to have to pull herself together before it was time to go to work, and the only way she could do that was to stop grieving and try to come to terms with the problem.

Grieving? Why had that word come to mind? Again she thought of Kenneth. Was she equating the loss of Rusty with the loss of her father?

No, that wasn't possible! She'd loved her dad, but she didn't love Rusty. He was just a friend. A special friend, maybe even a potential lover, but not in the same class as family. He couldn't be because she'd never have let that happen. She'd never allow herself to fall in love. Would she?

Annelise swallowed the last of the orange juice and got a cup for the coffee. It was strong and hot, and she carried it over to the Formica table and sat down. She'd been shocked literally speechless by Rusty's outburst and hasty departure last night and had had no chance to reason with him. All night long she'd been in such a state that she couldn't think, but he'd said he was leaving in a few days. She couldn't just let him walk out of her life the way her brother had, and, in a different way, her father had.

Rusty was big brother, father, friend and lover to her—all the roles a man filled in a woman's life—and now she was going to lose him, too, if she didn't act, and quickly.

By the time she left for work at nine-thirty, Annelise had thought of the perfect solution. If she could just track Rusty down and make him listen to her she knew he'd agree. Now all she had to do was persuade him to see her again.

When she got to the library she called his house, but no one answered the phone. She tried again at half-hour intervals until noon with the same results.

At twelve o'clock she locked up the library and walked across the highway to the business district. By law all employees were entitled to at least a half-hour for lunch. Usually Annelise brown-bagged it and ate at the table in the children's story section, which was always empty at that time of day, but this time she took her break and visited the four bars in the downtown area.

She walked into each one, looked around, bought a bag of pretzels or peanuts and left, but Rusty wasn't in any of them. She did see Maybelle Holden, though, at The Stockmen's Club during her last stop and was surprised to learn that Rusty's dancing partner was a bartender there.

Maybelle recognized Annelise first and greeted her. "Hi. Haven't seen you around lately. How are you?"

Annelise hadn't expected to find her behind the bar, but she smiled and returned the greeting. "Maybelle, it's nice to see you again. I didn't know you worked here."

The other woman grinned. "Been tending bar here for the past five years. Can I get you something?"

Annelise was caught off guard, and since this was her last stop she decided to relax for a few minutes. "Do you serve plain colas?"

"Sure, whatever you want." Maybelle scooped a glass in a bin of chipped ice, then held it under the fountain.

"Here you are," she said. "How about some peanuts or pretzels to go with it?"

Annelise already had several packages in her large purse, but she nodded and accepted another. She ripped this one open and poured the contents into her hand. "How can you tend bar and dance, too?" she asked,

remembering Maybelle's and Rusty's expertise on the
dance floor.

Maybelle's peal of laughter echoed through the nearly
empty room. "I don't work nights, especially Saturday
nights. It takes a strong, husky man to handle that
bunch come midnight or so. Is the library closed?
Haven't seen you in here during the day before."

Annelise sipped her cola and shook her head. "No,
but it's slow, so I locked up for the noon hour and took
off to get some fresh air and exercise."

She wondered if Maybelle knew where Rusty could be
reached but couldn't bring herself to ask. She didn't
want anyone to know she was looking for him. Instead
she asked, "Are you a native of Raindance?"

Again Maybelle's laughter brightened the room. It
was an easy, slightly bawdy sound that was infectious.
"Naw, I was born in Spearfish, South Dakota. Came to
this area about seven years ago with my ex-husband
when he got a job as mechanic at the Flying W ranch
out in the Sandhills. When the so-and-so took off
without me I got a job here as a barmaid and worked
my way up. Rusty says you're from Kansas City."

Annelise was amazed that the woman would talk
about her broken marriage so readily with a stranger.
On the other hand, since she'd brought Rusty's name
into the conversation, maybe Annelise could question
her after all.

"Yes, I was," she said. "By the way, have you seen
Rusty today? I need to get in touch with him."

Maybelle wiped at the bar with a towel. "Nope, but
he may be in later. You want me to tell him you're
lookin' for him?"

"No," Annelise said, and pushed her empty glass
aside. "It's not important." She slid off the stool and

put some dollar bills on the bar. "I've got to get back to work. It was nice talking to you."

Back at the library she tried again to call Rusty at home, but there was still no answer. A cold lump of dread settled in her stomach. Had he changed his mind and left town already? If so, it would be weeks before she could contact him. By then he'd have forgotten her.

An hour later when she called again with the same results her apprehension increased. Why hadn't she had her wits about her enough last night to think of the plan and the words that had come to her easily this morning? It was so simple, really. All she had to do was explain to Rusty how she felt, and he'd surely agree to her suggestion. Why did she always think of the perfect response after it was too late?

By three o'clock, two phone calls later, she was frantic. In her anxiety she'd misfiled several books on the shelves, forgotten to charge Mopsey Bradford the fine on her overdue novel and snapped at old Mr. Rogers, who was an eccentric pest but a taxpayer, nevertheless, and deserving of her polite attention.

She approached the telephone with dread. What was she going to do if Rusty really was gone? If he'd taken off thinking she agreed with his decision not to see her again?

When had he become so important to her that she couldn't face the thought of losing him? That was never supposed to have happened!

She took a deep breath, grabbed the phone and dialed. She felt nausea twist at her stomach as the bell on the other end rang, once, twice, three, four times. On the fifth ring there was a click and a deep voice growled, "Watt speaking."

Annelise was so relieved that she nearly dropped the instrument. She grabbed it and put it to her ear but then couldn't speak.

Rusty didn't have the same problem. "Hello, this is Rusty Watt. It's your nickel, so say something."

She finally managed to catch her breath. "Rusty." It had an odd, choking sound.

There was a moment's pause. "Annelise?" He sounded a little choked up, too.

"Oh, Rusty, I—I was so afraid.... I've tried and tried to get you...." She knew she wasn't making sense.

"Annelise, what's the matter?" Rusty's tone had gone from breathless to gruff. "Answer me, are you all right?"

"I'm fine now." She finally got her breathing regulated and sounded almost normal. "I was so afraid you'd left—"

He cleared his throat. "What is it you want?"

Apparently he wasn't glad to hear from her. Well, he'd made his wishes clear. What did she expect?

"I want to see you. I need to talk to you."

Again there was a pause. "Damn it, Annelise, I told you—"

"I know," she interrupted hurriedly, "but you didn't give me a chance to respond."

"There was no response required," he grated.

He sounded so cold and uninterested. Was she being dense? Had he simply tired of her and tried to tell her so without hurting her feelings? That's the way Rusty would handle it. For all his size and chauvinistic ways he was gentle and kind, except when he lost his temper. Well, either way she had to know.

"Yes there was. Please, Rusty, it's important to me." She couldn't keep her voice from quivering.

She heard him sigh. "All right, where and when do you want to meet?"

She was having second thoughts. Maybe this wasn't such a good idea after all. She'd always disapproved of clinging women who chased after men. But surely she wasn't doing that. If the excuse Rusty had given her for breaking off their friendship was true, then he would be happy to hear what she had to say. Wouldn't he?

"If...if you'd like to come over to the house this evening I'll fix dinner. We can—"

"No, Annelise." His tone left no room for argument. "I'm not coming there, and you're not coming here. You know what happens every time we get together at your place or mine. Wait for me at the library. I'll meet you at six o'clock and we can talk there."

He hung up before she could agree.

By six o'clock Annelise was a nervous wreck, and when Rusty walked in looking like the movies version of a cowboy, her pulse skyrocketed and her heart sped up so fast that she could hardly breathe. He frowned at her and made no move to take off either his Stetson or his sheepskin jacket.

She locked the door, then made a massive effort to smile. "Thank you for coming," she said as she walked toward a study table and chairs. "Come on over here and sit down."

"I prefer to stand." There was no yielding in his tone as he moved closer but kept a sizable distance between them.

How could she broach the intimate subject she needed to talk about when he was being so unapproachable? She wished he'd sit and unbend a little, then maybe she could relax, too, but she didn't want the disadvantage of sitting while he was standing. Obviously he wasn't going to make this easy for her, so she might as well begin.

She squared her shoulders and looked at him. "I—I don't want to lose you, Rusty. Last night you said I was dear to you. Well, you're dear to me, too. I—I've come to rely on your friendship and support." She smiled. "Yes, and even your protection. I guess I'm not as independent as I thought."

He jammed his hands in his pockets and turned away. "I also said I wasn't going to see you again, and I expected you to respect my decision."

She leaned against the bookshelf for support before her trembling knees gave way. "But you indicated that you wanted to make love to me." Her voice was low and husky. "I want you, too. You're the only man I've ever wanted that way, and I'd like you to be my first lover."

There, it was out, and she closed her eyes so she wouldn't have to see his reaction.

"Why?" He spit the word out, terse and cold.

That wasn't the reaction she'd expected, and her lids flew open to reveal him turned again to face her, his expression hard and inscrutable.

"Why? Well, I . . . I like you, and you'd be a gentle and patient teacher."

As soon as the words were out she regretted them. It sounded so clinical, and that wasn't at all the way she'd meant it.

"I—I mean just because neither of us is ready for marriage doesn't mean we can't be lovers. I never intended to remain a virgin, if that's what's bothering you. It's just that I never before met a man I wanted to make love with."

His eyes narrowed to slits. "Would you want to live with me?"

She blinked. "Oh, no... I mean people would talk. We... we could be... intimate... without being blatant about it."

She'd clenched her hands together and was twisting her fingers. Oh, for heaven's sake! She was talking like a ninny. She wasn't doing this right at all.

He nodded. "I see. I'm not polished and sophisticated enough to be considered your *constant companion*," he made the term sound obscene, "but I qualify as a part-time stud as long as no one knows how far you've lowered your standards. In other words you want to have a furtive, short-term affair with me until something better comes along." His voice crackled with rage.

The color drained from Annelise's face, and she felt light-headed. She was horrified that Rusty had so misunderstood her. Dear God, it had all seemed so reasonable when she'd planned it, but when she'd tried to put it into words it came out sounding cheap and degrading.

"No!" she shouted, and leaned more heavily against the bookshelf. "You don't understand!"

"Oh, but I do." His tone was dangerously low and calm. "I misjudged you at first, but now I understand you better than you understand yourself. You're a barracuda, Annelise. Graceful and pretty on the outside, but dangerous and destructive underneath. You'll tear men apart for your own selfish purposes, then throw them away when they're no longer useful to you. Sorry, but I'm not quite the country rube you mistook me for.

You'll have to find some other sucker to sharpen your teeth on.''

He turned and stomped to the outside door, then slammed it behind him.

Chapter Nine

A loud banging on a door woke Annelise with a start, and she gazed around her with confusion. What was she doing sleeping at a table in the library?

"Miss Kelsey, are you in there?" a gruff male voice shouted, and the banging started again.

She jumped up and rushed to open the door. A man in a heavy blue uniform jacket and cap to match, whom she recognized as Ox Jennings, the sheriff, stepped inside. "Sorry if I scared you," he said, "but when I drove by and saw the light was still on I figured I'd better check." He squinted at her. "Is anything the matter?"

The cold air swept away the cobwebs of her mind, and she knew why he looked concerned. Her face and eyes must be bloated and red from the marathon crying session she'd indulged in before apparently falling asleep sitting on the hard chair with her head cradled in her arms on the wooden table.

She shook her head and tried to smile. "No, nothing's wrong. I stayed late to catch up on some work and must have fallen asleep. I'll be leaving as soon as I get my coat."

The sheriff stood his ground. "I'll wait and drive you home. It's after ten o'clock, and the temperature's well below freezing."

Within a few minutes Annelise was home and had turned the thermostat up to take the chill off the house. Her head throbbed, and her stomach felt queasy. In an effort to keep her mind off Rusty and his crushingly painful accusation she went into the kitchen and made coffee. While it was perking she remembered that she hadn't eaten since lunch the day before, so she fixed a tuna sandwich and carried it and the coffee into the living room where she could relax in the lounge chair.

It didn't happen. Although the chair was comfortable, her nerves were tense and Rusty's angry voice seemed to bounce off the walls. *You're a barracuda...barracuda...barracuda. You tear men apart...apart...apart. Selfish...selfish...selfish.*

"No!" Her cry mingled with the words in her mind, and she curled up in a ball and clasped her hands over her ears in a futile effort to shut them out. She wasn't like that. She'd never hurt Rusty.

But she had hurt him, and deeply, or he'd never have torn into her the way he had, battering her with words and throwing her offer of love back in her face.

She raised her head and lowered her hands to lie in her lap. Love? No, she hadn't offered him love. Love would bind her, melt away her freedom and make her a captive. She couldn't offer Rusty love because then she'd belong to him.

She leaned her aching head against the back of the chair as a nagging little voice somewhere deep inside her whispered, *But that's what you want, isn't it? You want to belong to Rusty, to have him belong to you. To live with him, love him, bear his children.*

She closed her eyes. Oh, my God. She was in love with Rusty! How could she have been so blind? So insensitive to her own feelings?

She rubbed her hands over her face. She'd been blithely prattling on every time they were together about her cherished independence, her hard-won education, the dream man she'd eventually marry. No wonder Rusty was so disgusted with her that he'd go to almost any lengths to get rid of her.

Now that she thought back she remembered that it was after she'd first told him that she'd only marry a rich man and never for love that he began trying to distance himself from her. Even so, he'd been jealous of her dates with Lance, and when they were alone together he'd seemed compelled to touch her, kiss her, hold her.

She'd responded like a torch to a flame, but still she'd told herself that she couldn't be in love with him because he didn't match the cardboard image of her rich Prince Charming. Hell, whatever made her think she was Cinderella?

All the time she'd been falling in love and was too stubborn to admit it. Had Rusty been falling in love with her, too?

She jumped up, and the plate and two halves of her sandwich went flying in all directions. Muttering unladylike curses she picked them up and paced around the room.

Was she selfishly using men? Beckoning them with one hand while pushing them away with the other?

No. Never. She paused in her pacing. At least, never before Rusty. With him? Yes, it was possible. Maybe it was selfish of her to want financial security rather than love, but she'd grown up with the example of her mother who'd gone through so much hell in the name of love.

Still, Rusty wasn't like her father. Rusty was a strong man, a man who'd never let those who depended on him down. She knew that for a fact. She had only to remember how he'd been there for her, a total stranger, when she'd needed someone so badly.

She sank back down in the chair. He'd been so thoughtful, so tender. A tower of strength when her own had deserted her. She'd fallen in love with him before she left the hospital, but she hadn't had the maturity to recognize her dream man because he wore jeans instead of suits and drank beer instead of champagne.

She groaned with despair. Had she lost any chance she may have had with Rusty? He'd been so hurt and so indignant, and with good reason.

Her cheeks burned with shame. She'd been so rattled by his coldness that she'd said all the wrong things without realizing how they'd sound. Had she killed all hope of getting him to listen to an apology? Of making him believe her, or even care, if she told him she loved him?

The night wore on, and Annelise's mind continued its merciless tirade. She'd never felt so desolate and alone. Maybe her mother was right. Wasn't it better to make mistakes and grope toward the elusive state called happiness with someone you loved than to walk frigidly through life alone, untouched and unwanted?

At least Sandra Kelsey had been loved and needed. Annelise remembered times over the years, after her parents had quarreled about her father's drinking and broken promises, when she'd inadvertently come across them later crying in each other's arms. Kenneth was always pleading with Sandra not to leave him, because without her he'd be truly lost. Sandra had always stayed. Maybe she knew that loving too much was better than not loving at all.

Finally, in the cold, dark hours of early morning, Annelise came to a conclusion. She had to go to Rusty and tell him of her love. Even though he'd made it plain that he never wanted to have anything more to do with her, that she'd killed whatever tender feelings he may have had for her, she couldn't bear to let him believe that she'd only been using him. Somehow she had to make him listen to her.

At three-forty-five she stumbled into the bedroom and crawled into bed without even removing her clothes. Within minutes she was asleep.

The jarring ring of the telephone woke her out of a deep slumber, and she rolled out of bed and hurried across the small, square hallway that separated the bedroom and bathroom from the kitchen and dining room. She answered the phone in the kitchen, and it was her neighbor, Rosemarie Perkins.

"I just had a call from Bryce Garrett," she said, too excited to start the conversation by saying hello. "He says Carol's having contractions and he's taking her to the hospital."

Annelise felt a twinge of unease. "But she's not due yet. Is everything all right?"

"Oh sure, it's only about ten days early, and when she saw Dr. Cole last week he said the baby was in position and could come anytime. Bryce promised to keep us informed. Why don't you come over for coffee and wait with us? We're not going to church, Billy has a cold."

Annelise looked at her watch. It was almost eleven o'clock! How could she have slept so late? "Oh golly, Rosie, I wish I could, but I've got to find Rusty."

Rosemarie chuckled. "What do you mean 'find' Rusty? He's seldom very far away from you."

A surge of despair replaced the happiness of learning that her dear friend Carol's baby was imminent. "I wish that were true." She could hear the wistfulness in her tone. "But we quarreled last night, and he made it pretty plain that he didn't want to see me anymore. I'm afraid he meant it, but even so I've got to find him and tell him how much I love him."

It occurred to her that ordinarily she'd never confide such a thing to anyone, but now she needed to talk and Rosie was a sympathetic listener. "He's going away soon," she continued, "and will be gone for a couple of months. I've got to talk to him before he leaves." Her voice broke, and she pressed her lips together to hold back a sob.

"I'm sorry, honey," Rosemarie said gently. "Is there anything I can do?"

Annelise thought for a moment. "Yes, would you mind calling his house and letting me know whether or not he's home. He won't stay around if he knows I'm looking for him, but it's so cold and windy that I hate to walk over if he's not there."

Rosemarie readily agreed and hung up, only to call back a few minutes later with good news. "He's there. I told him about Carol going to the hospital, and he said he'd be home most of the day and to be sure to let him know when the baby comes. Good luck. Don't leave until he asks you to marry him.''

Fat chance, Annelise thought. ''I'd marry him tomorrow, but I'm afraid there's not much hope for that.'' Again she swallowed a sob. ''I really messed up this time, but thanks for your help. I'll talk to you later.''

Annelise quickly showered and dressed in purple sweatpants and a matching zippered sweatshirt with mauve trim. The color looked especially good on her, but even so her white face showed the ravages of the past two nights. There were shadows under her puffy eyes, but she didn't want to waste time on an elaborate makeup camouflage. She applied lipstick and tied a mauve scarf around her head to hold back the long hair that took too much time to braid.

She was dressed and out of the house in twenty minutes. Even with warm clothes under her quilted parka the north wind seemed to whip the cold right through her, making her shiver. She walked fast and hoped the brisk pace and the cold breeze would put a little color in her gaunt face. The last thing she wanted was for Rusty to feel sorry for her.

By the time she rounded the corner on Rusty's street, she was practically running and she slowed down and tried to still her hammering heart. She was vaguely aware of a bright red foreign sports car parked at the curb in front of his house as she turned up the walkway to the porch, but she was too nervous and preoccupied to notice.

She knocked, then stood quavering as she heard footsteps approaching the door. When it opened she stared with surprise. The man was nearly as big as

Rusty, but he had black hair and wore navy-blue wool slacks and a light blue dress shirt open at the neck.

For a moment he looked almost as startled as she, then his face split in a big smile and he opened the storm door to admit her. "Well, hello there," he boomed. "If you're looking for Rusty he's under the shower, but he'll be out in a minute. Come on in, for God's sake, it's too cold to stand out there."

"Oh, I . . . I . . ." Good heavens, Rusty had company. She'd have to come back some other time.

Before she could complete her sentence or move, the man took her arm and pulled her forward. "Come on, your teeth are chattering. I won't bite."

He had her inside before she could protest. "I'm Quinn Downing, from Cheyenne," he said, in a voice that she suspected would carry even if he whispered. "I just stopped in to say hello to Rusty on my way to Omaha. We were roommates at Stanford."

Annelise's eyes widened. "Stanford?"

"Yeah, you know, Stanford University? California? Let's get you out of that jacket—it's nice and warm in here."

He reached out and began undoing the rather complicated fastenings on her parka, as though she were a child who had to be helped.

She pulled away. "I can do it," she said firmly, and had slipped the parka off before she remembered that she wasn't going to stay.

He took it and tossed it over the arm of the sofa, then looked at her thoroughly but without offense. "Hey, I didn't know they grew such pretty little gals on this godforsaken prairie. What's your name?"

Annelise was still trying to take in the fact that this man and Rusty Watt had been roommates *at Stanford* and answered without thinking. "Annelise Kelsey. Mr. Downing. I can't stay—"

"Quinn," he said firmly, "and it's *Dr.* Downing, thanks to Mr. and Mrs. Watt."

Annelise wondered if she was losing her mind. Nothing the man said seemed to make sense to her. "Rusty's parents?"

Quinn nodded. "They put me through veterinary school after my dad lost everything through a series of bad investments in our senior year of college—"

"Quinn!" Rusty's voice, harsh and impatient, interrupted his friend.

He was standing in the archway between the living and dining rooms, and the look on his face was one of shock and displeasure.

"Aw, come on, Rusty. Don't be so modest. You know damn well that if your folks hadn't footed the bills I'd never have been able to get into U.C. Davis."

Quinn turned to Annelise. "That's the best veterinary school in the country, but it's also probably the most expensive. I owe those generous people more than I can ever repay, and I don't mean money. There's not many who'd put out that kind of cash for a kid who's not even a relative. Especially after sending their own three brilliant sons through Stanford. Did Rusty tell you he graduated in the top ten percent of his class and played football, too?"

The room began to spin, and Annelise sat down quickly on the sofa behind her. What was wrong with this blustery, talkative man? He had the names right, but he wasn't referring to the same people she knew. He was implying that Rusty and his family were rich and well-educated, but that wasn't true. Rusty drove a truck and his parents and brothers worked on a ranch.

She looked up and saw Rusty watching her from across the room, his expression grim; but Quinn rambled on, obviously unaware of the tension. "Hey, pal, remember the first time I visited you at the ranch? You took me for a ride around all 80,000 or so acres, and I couldn't believe that even the Watt family could own so much land."

He sat down on the couch beside Annelise, but continued his nonstop talking. "And the cattle! Thousands of whitefaced Herefords, Angus, and several exotic breeds, fat and ready for market. Hell, I was born and raised in San Francisco. My idea of a ranch was a hundred acres with maybe eight or ten cows." He laughed heartily, then sobered. "Hey, I'm sorry. You came to see Rusty, and I'm doing all the talking."

Annelise was devastated. This Quinn Downing was telling her that Rusty had graduated with honors from one of the most prestigious and expensive private colleges, and that he and his family were not only well-off financially but actually wealthy!

She felt like a prize fool.

Had Rusty deliberately set her up, or had he just stood by and let her do it all by herself? Either way he must have been laughing at her, enjoying her silly, juvenile performance right from the beginning.

How could he? He'd been so kind and protective. He'd really seemed to care about her.

On the other hand, why shouldn't he take advantage of her self-righteous protestations? Without meaning to she'd insulted him time and time again with her snobbish little jabs at his occupation and his so-called lack of refinement.

She had to get out of here. In a few minutes she was going to fall apart, and she couldn't bear to have either

Rusty or his friend know how excruciatingly she'd been hurt.

Praying that her trembling legs would hold her, she stood and almost bumped into Rusty who'd come across the room toward her.

"Annelise," he said, and caught her by the upper arms.

She cringed as though he'd struck her, and with a sharp intake of breath he released her and stepped back.

"I really have to leave," she said as she picked up her parka and, without looking at either man, headed toward the door. "It was nice meeting you, Dr. Downing," she called out without turning.

She reached for the knob, but Rusty's hand was already there. "I'll drive you home," he said, and his voice sounded strange, almost as strangled as hers.

"No!" She pulled her hand back and recoiled. "I'd rather walk. I need the exercise."

"Then put your jacket on," he said, still holding the door shut.

Oh God, couldn't she do anything right? She'd have run out into the freezing cold without even a coat.

Rusty took the jacket from her and held it while she slipped into it, careful not to touch him. "If you don't want me to drive you then let Quinn do it." He raised the hood and settled it on her head, pushing strands of long blond hair back in the process. "Where are your gloves?"

She almost cried out with frustration as she took them from her pockets and began pulling them on. She couldn't really blame him for treating her like an idiot child—she was behaving like one—but she'd so badly wanted to make a dignified exit.

"I prefer to walk," she said more forcefully this time. "If you'll please open the door?"

She could feel his gaze on her even though she couldn't bring herself to look at him. Then he opened the door and allowed her to escape.

Annelise was aware of the biting wind that stung her cheeks and whipped around her sweatpants-clad legs, but instead of turning west at the end of the street that would have taken her home, she turned east and walked away. She couldn't face going back to the house right now. She needed the cold stimulant of the weather, and the activity of walking.

Her whole future had just crashed down around her. There was no way she could tell Rusty that she loved him now. Even if there were a chance that he wanted to hear it, which there wasn't, he'd never believe her. He'd be sure she was only after his money.

Is that why he'd kept his background such a big secret? Yes, of course it was. He was afraid she'd try to seduce him into marrying her and becoming the rich "stud" who would provide her with children and financial security.

Her face burned, but not with the cold. She was humiliated that he'd think so badly of her, and appalled that she had no one to blame but herself.

She was feeling shaky and light-headed when she came to a barren field and realized that she'd walked all the way to the eastern outskirts of town and was about two blocks in back of the Raindance Inn motel on the highway. She knew the Steak and Stein next to the Inn, and it occurred to her that she had eaten practically nothing since lunch on Friday. No wonder she felt weak and dizzy.

She made her way to the restaurant where she settled into a small booth in a corner and ordered cream of broccoli soup and a turkey, ham and bacon club sandwich. It was warm in the restaurant, and she took off her jacket before starting on her thick, hot soup. By the time she'd finished the sandwich and a cup of steaming black tea she felt stronger, calmer and better able to cope.

Outside again she headed south toward the hospital. After inquiring at the admissions desk she was told that Carol Garrett was still in labor but everything was progressing normally and the baby would probably be born in another hour or two. She bought a card in the small gift shop in the lobby and wrote a short but loving message of encouragement and asked that it be delivered to Carol and Bryce in her room.

When she left the hospital she turned north, then west toward Main Street, but by the time she got to the high school she was tired and panting for breath against the wind. She remembered the little bench in the alcove where she and Lance had come during half-time on Thanksgiving to talk, and she found it and sank wearily down on the hard, rough wood.

It was sheltered from the wind, and she brought her legs up, wrapped her arms around her shins and put her face on her knees. This was a favorite position when she was burdened with more problems than she could handle. She'd learned in psychology class that it had a prenatal back-to-the-womb-wish significance, and that sounded reasonable. At no other time in their lives were human beings so well protected and safe. It was only natural that they'd subconsciously long for a return to that state when the going got rough.

What was she going to do now? For twenty-two years she'd avoided the hazards of falling in love. She'd never even experienced the teenage crushes that were part of a young girl's growing up, having had neither the time nor the inclination. It was no wonder she hadn't recognized love when it had quietly invaded her heart and soul.

There was no longer any doubt that Rusty had meant what he said. He didn't want her as a friend, or a lover, and certainly not as a wife. If she hadn't been so busy protecting herself from imaginary future problems she might have had a chance with him, but in her fear and resulting clumsiness she'd killed whatever feelings he'd had for her.

She knew she'd never love another man with the same passionate intensity, but she'd make no further attempt to explain or apologize to Rusty. All she had left was a small amount of pride, and she desperately needed it to cling to. Making a pest of herself would get her nowhere and only embarrass them both.

Annelise had been huddled on the bench for a long time, agonizing over her failures and trying to come up with some sort of cohesive plan for the future, when she heard the sound of heavy footsteps on the walkway a few feet from her sheltered hideaway. She lifted her head from its resting place on her upraised knees just as Rusty came around a low hedge and walked toward her.

Chapter Ten

Neither Annelise nor Rusty spoke until he sat down on the bench beside her. His face had a pinched look, and his hazel eyes were hooded. "I've been looking for you," he said, and she noticed that his fists were clenched on his jeans-covered thighs.

"Oh?" She put her legs down and planted her feet firmly on the cement.

"Nobody knew where you'd gone." There was a tremor in his tone, but she could tell that he was trying to conceal it.

"I—I didn't feel like going home, so I decided to walk around." She folded her gloved hands in her lap and wondered why she felt so numb.

"In this cold wind? It's been hours since you left my house." He drew the leather glove off his right hand and put the back of the hand against her flushed cheek. "Your cheek's like ice and you're shivering."

Her brown eyes widened, and in spite of the cold his hand felt warm on her skin. "It's protected from the wind here, and I wasn't aware of the cold until you mentioned it." She wished her voice was more vibrant. It sounded so flat and lifeless.

"You'll catch pneumonia if you stay outside any longer." He took her hand in his, then stood, pulling her up with him. "Come, Annelise," he said softly. "Let's go home."

Her knees were stiff from being bent in an unnatural position for so long, and she stumbled as she started to walk. Rusty put his arm around her waist and supported her until they got to his Bronco, which was parked at the curb.

The heater had been running and the vehicle was warm, but she still shivered as they drove along the blacktop residential streets. "How did you know where I was? You couldn't have seen me from the car." She didn't look at him but stared straight ahead.

He didn't look at her, either. "I called Lance Farr to see if you were with him. He said it was none of my business. I said I was looking for you, and he indicated that I should go to hell. I told him that's where I was calling from, that you'd run away from me and I was nearly out of mind trying to find you. He suggested that I'd probably brought it on myself, which I admitted, but after casting doubts about my parentage he remembered the little alcove in the school building and advised me to try there. His last words to me were a threat that he'd render me unable to consummate a marriage or father children if anything had happened to you. He meant it, too."

Annelise couldn't help laughing at his delicate translation of Lance's apparently obscene remarks. "Lance is a dear, sweet friend."

"Yes." He snapped the word off short as he pulled into the driveway of his house.

"I thought you were going to take me home," she said.

"I have." He got out of the Bronco and went around to help her.

Inside the house he quickly removed his jacket and hat, then turned to her. "You're so cold your teeth are chattering." His tone was harsh as he began unbuttoning her parka. "We've got to get you under a hot shower before you get sick."

"Shower?" It was almost a yelp. "I'm not going to shower here. I want you to take me home."

He slid the jacket off her arms and let it drop to the floor, then reached for the long zipper on her sweatshirt. "You can either take those clothes off yourself or I'll do it for you."

She gasped and reached out to stay his hand as he pulled at the zipper. He grinned. "I was hoping you'd let me do it, but have it your way. Now scoot, and stay under the shower until you're warm all the way through."

There were stacks of heavy oversize towels and washcloths in the linen closet, and Annelise stood under the hot shower until the room was thick with steam and the hot water was rapidly cooling. Nothing had ever felt so good as the heat that slowly penetrated the block of ice she had become.

She turned off the water and groped through the steam for the towels she'd placed on the clothes hamper. After toweling her long hair with one and drying herself with the other, she put on her panties and had just reached for her bra when there was a knock at the door and Rusty called, "Open up, I have something for you."

Standing behind the door, she opened it enough for him to hand her her own fuzzy yellow robe and slippers. "Where did you get these?" she asked as she reached for them.

"I took your keys out of your purse and went over to your house and got them. I have hot chocolate when you're ready for it."

She quickly belted the warm robe around her and slipped her feet into the furry slippers, then tied a dry towel turban-style around her still damp hair.

In the kitchen Rusty poured fragrant chocolate milk into ironstone mugs and added a marshmallow to each. He looked up when Annelise came in, and for a moment their gazes collided and clung. She thought she saw a mixture of anguish and longing in his, but he looked away before she could be sure.

"Feeling better?" he asked as he handed her one of the mugs.

"Much," she said, "and, Rusty, thank you for taking such good care of me."

She definitely saw him wince, but before she could say anything he headed out of the kitchen. "Come on," he said over his shoulder, "we have to talk, but we might as well be comfortable while we're doing it."

She followed him into the living room where she sat down on the sofa, and he chose the big leather recliner. She took a sip of her hot chocolate and wondered nervously what he wanted to talk about. He'd surely said everything he had to say last night at the library. If he was going to bawl her out for coming over here this morning and then running away and being discourteous to his friend, she didn't think she could stand it.

Her hand shook, and she set her mug down on the end table before she could spill it. She glanced across at Rusty and saw that he'd put his mug down, too, and was sitting uneasily on the edge of the chair with his arms resting on his thighs.

He was the first to speak, although he still didn't look at her. "Annelise, I'm sorry I misled you about my background and my...my financial situation. And I'm especially sorry that you found out the way you did."

Her eyes widened with surprise. He wasn't scolding her, he was apologizing!

She swallowed and hoped her voice wouldn't break. "It—it came as quite a shock. At first I was really hurt, but then I realized that it was my own fault. I hadn't even asked you about your schooling or your parents. I'd just made blind assumptions based on nothing more than the fact that you drove a truck, dressed in jeans all the time and drank beer. You didn't owe me anything, Rusty. You still don't. I'm the one who is indebted to you. You were always there when I needed you the most and I...I repaid you by making wrong assumptions and insulting you."

She dropped her face in her hands and her voice was choked with repressed sobs. "Oh, Rusty, I never, ever meant to insult you or hurt you. I was so afraid I'd fall in love with you that I said things I didn't mean without realizing how it sounded."

He bounded out of the chair and sat down beside her on the sofa, then lifted her onto his lap and held her close. "Don't cry, sweetheart. Oh, God, I can't stand it if you cry." His voice was harsh with torment. "I've just about reached the end of my endurance. I spent the whole night pacing the floor and telling myself there was no way I was going to take you on your terms, but by morning I knew I had to have you. I was planning to go to you, tell you the truth about myself and agree to anything you wanted if you'd just marry me and let me love you.''

Annelise gasped but he didn't seem to notice. ''Then Quinn showed up unexpectedly and I was delayed. When I walked out of the shower and saw you sitting in my living room looking so pale and shocked and betrayed, while he prattled on telling you all the things I should have and didn't, I could have throttled him.''

Annelise's mind was reeling. She struggled to push herself far enough away that she could look at him, and he reluctantly loosened his hold. ''Just a minute,'' she said anxiously. ''Back up a little. Did you say you were going to ask me to marry you?''

He nodded soberly and placed a chaste kiss on her trembling lips. ''I think I qualify for your specification of a rich man. A lot of the family fortune is tied up in land and cattle, but I'll have Bryce draw up a prenuptial agreement guaranteeing you the security you need.''

She should have been estatic, but instead she could have cried. He was prepared to buy her because that's what he thought she wanted from him! Would she ever be able to make him believe the truth?

She threw her arms around his neck and rubbed her wet cheek against him. ''Oh, darling,'' she murmured brokenly. ''I don't want your money. The reason I came over here this morning was to tell you that I love you, and I want to marry you. That if you want to drive a truck, drink beer and dance like a cowboy, that's fine with me. All my life I've budgeted carefully, so it wouldn't be a problem—although it apparently won't be necessary—but I will keep the fridge stocked with beer, polish your pointed-toe boots and learn to like country music."

She hesitated, then continued shyly. "I'll also keep you happy in bed for as long as we both shall live."

It was only when she finished talking that she realized he was no longer cuddling her but was tense and unresponsive in her arms.

"Rusty?" She kissed him just below the ear. "What's the matter?"

"Don't lie to me, Annelise." It was a cry of pain. "It's not necessary to pretend that you love me. We both know your feelings on that subject."

Again he clasped her tightly to him. "The reason I didn't tell you about the ranch and my extensive education was because I was afraid that would make me attractive husband material, and I knew that if you set out to marry me I'd never be able to resist you. I didn't think I could bear having you and knowing you'd only married me for my money, but by this morning I knew that even that would be better than not having you at all."

Annelise groaned with frustration as she stroked her fingers through his clean, thick hair. "I'm not lying! I know I said all those stupid things about marrying for money and children instead of love, but—"

"Don't." He held her away from him and looked at her. "You've always been truthful with me, even when it was embarrassing or hurtful for you, so please don't stop now. I know you're trying to spare me, but that's not necessary. We'll be happy together—how can we help but be? I can be the kind of husband you want, and just having you for my wife and all that implies will give me joy beyond description. There's more passion between us than we have a right to hope for now, and maybe someday you'll learn to love me."

Annelise was frantic. How could she have gotten into such an untenable situation? She couldn't stand to have Rusty think she was only pretending to love him. Maybe, over a period of months, she could show him how very deeply she cared, but in the meantime he'd be miserable thinking the only thing she wanted from him was security.

She took his brooding face between her hands and kissed him, tenderly at first but then with rising passion. With a low moan he cradled her against him and she parted her lips to allow him the entry he sought. His hand found her bare breast beneath her robe and cupped it as she unfastened the buttons of his heavy flannel shirt and felt the warmth of his chest beneath her palm.

"I don't want you to change anything about yourself," she whispered against his eager mouth. "I fell in love with you just the way you are. I didn't know there were men like you in the world. If I had I'd never have gotten so confused as to think love was a form of bondage."

He lowered his head and pushed aside the furry material of her robe, then kissed the breast he was holding, sending shivers up her spine. "You'll like me better in a suit and tie." He shifted his attention to the other breast. "I even own a tuxedo. I'll wear it for you on the opening night of the opera. Do you prefer the Metropolitan or the San Francisco company?"

To attend an opera at the Metropolitan Opera House had always been one of her fondest dreams, but now that it was within reach she realized that it was way down at the bottom on her list of priorities. "Oh,

Rusty." Her voice was ragged with despair as she clasped his face against her soft, warm flesh. "How can I make you understand? What can I do to make you believe me?"

"You can like me, respect me and keep on responding so enthusiastically when we make love," he said patiently. "No man could expect more, my darling. I have enough love in me for both of us. We'll do just fine."

But they wouldn't. Not if he thought she was only accommodating him. That wasn't fair. Not to him—but not to her, either. He'd always think she was pretending, and she'd be under enormous pressure to prove that she wasn't. It was an intolerable situation, but she didn't know how to correct it.

Her robe had fallen away, exposing her legs, and he put his hand on her bare thigh, sending waves of heat coursing through her. She shuddered and cuddled closer when the clang of the telephone broke the spell.

Rusty swore lustily. "I'd better answer it," he said, and set her off his lap. "I have some nosy friends who are apt to come looking for me if they can't rouse me on the phone."

The ringing continued, and he stood and pulled her up with him. "Come on," he said and put his arm around her as he propelled them toward the bedroom. "I'm not going to take any chances that you'll run off again."

"You couldn't get rid of me if you tried," she assured him, as she readjusted her loosened robe while he picked up the phone.

"Watt speaking. Oh, hi, Rosemarie.... No kidding, that's great!... Hold on a minute, I want to tell Annelise." He turned to her with a big smile on his face.

"Carol and Bryce have a baby son. Six pounds, fourteen ounces," he announced happily, then spoke again into the phone. "Yeah, she's here. What do you mean 'congratulations'? How did you know?"

Annelise felt a warm burst of radiance. Rosemarie Perkins! Of course! Why didn't she think of Rosie sooner?

She tugged at Rusty's sleeve. "Rusty, I want you to ask her something."

He looked at her, puzzled. "Just a minute, Rosie," he said, then put his hand over the mouthpiece.

"Tell her I said to tell you everything I said to her this morning." Annelise was almost dancing with excitement.

"What?" He apparently thought she'd lost her mind.

"Just go ahead and do it," she urged.

He shrugged, then repeated what she'd said into the telephone. He listened a moment, then looked again at Annelise. She says 'everything?'"

"Yes, absolutely everything. Tell her to repeat it word for word if she can remember."

He relayed the message, then listened. She saw him stiffen and his eyes widen. "She said that?"

Another pause, then, "Are you sure? Maybe you misunderstood."

More pausing, then his face lit up with sheer happiness. "Bless you, my friend," he said fervently. "We'll name our first daughter after you. That's a promise."

He slammed down the phone and swept her into his arms. "She said that early this morning before you came over here you told her that you loved me and wanted to marry me." His big smile momentarily dimmed, and he looked straight into her soul. "Is that the honest truth, Annelise?"

Solemnly she met his gaze. "I swear on everything I hold dear." She moved into his arms. "Oh, darling, I love you so much."

He kissed her then and set off fireworks of pure joy between them. With a few deft movements they were lying on the bed. Without taking his mouth from hers Rusty unfastened the belt to Annelise's robe and caressed her overheated body with his big but gentle hand. She pulled his shirt out of his jeans and delighted in the feel of his strong, muscular back, and the way those muscles twitched as her palms rubbed over them.

For a long time they said nothing as their fingers and their lips explored and teased and pleasured. Finally, Rusty pulled back and covered Annelise with the folds of her robe.

She looked up at him in confusion, and he smiled and kissed the tip of her nose. "It's time to stop, sweetheart." His tone was raspy with need. "I'm not going to spoil our wedding night for you, but have mercy and set the date sometime this month."

She would never have stopped him, but even though her body protested the interruption, she felt both loved and honored. She reached up and stroked his face. "Is two weeks from today soon enough? That's the weekend before Christmas."

Suddenly she remembered something he'd told her and she sat up, appalled. "Rusty, you won't be here then! You said you were leaving next week and would be gone for two months." The dismay and disappointment that swept through her were almost crushing.

Rusty pulled her back down and kissed the breast that had been exposed by her hasty movements. "No problem, darlin'." His hand settled on her once-more-bare leg. "I'll just cancel and let someone else have the job.

There's one thing you need to know, though. I'm not going to be a truck jockey anymore."

Annelise frowned. "Rusty, I told you, I love you exactly the way you are, and that includes your freewheeling life-style. You don't have to give it up for me."

He chuckled. "Honey, if you think I'm going to leave you at home in bed alone while I roam all over the country you're just plain demented. Once this union of ours is blessed by church and state we're going to spend every night together for the rest of our lives. Besides, you'll need me around to help with the kids."

Her mouth quirked in amusement. "The kids?"

"You said you wanted children, didn't you?"

She nodded. "How many do you plan on giving me?"

His expression was serious, but his eyes twinkled with laughter. "Oh, let's see. You're awfully young. We should be able to turn them out at the rate of about one a year for the next fifteen or twenty years."

Annelise shrieked and hit him with one of the bed pillows. Rusty captured her arms and held them over her head as he kissed her, long and thoroughly. "Will you settle for two kids and the career you've always dreamed of?" There was no teasing in his tone now.

Annelise felt a fleeting regret for her plans to continue her education and work in a big important library. "I guess they can always use me here in Raindance," she said.

He rolled onto his back and pulled her over to lie on top of him. "We won't be living in Raindance, love. I've always intended to someday have my own trucking company. I should have started it long ago, but I never had any reason to settle down before. There's no reason why you can't get your master's degree—a doctorate, too—and work wherever you want. I can set up a trucking business anywhere. Just pick a city that has a good university and a library you like, and we'll move there."

Annelise was overwhelmed by his thoughtfulness and generosity. She murmured, "I love you," but the lump in her throat rendered her nearly incoherent so she proceeded to show him.

As their lovemaking heated up again, Rusty rolled them over so that he was lying partially across her, ravaging her willing mouth. When they finally had to breathe he broke away with a muttered oath and scrambled off the bed.

She watched, fascinated, as he reached out and lifted her to her feet beside him, then pulled her robe tightly around her and knotted the belt. "Annelise Kelsey," he grated, "go put your clothes on. And no matter what I say or do, you leave them on when you're around me for the next two weeks. Understood?"

She grinned. "Yes, sir." She turned and took a couple of steps toward the hall, then looked over her shoulder. "Does that mean even if you beg?"

He glared at her. "Yes."

"And plead?"

His mouth twitched with amusement. "Of course."

She turned to face him again. "But you know I've never been able to say no to you," she said plaintively.

He closed the gap between them and taking her hands brought them to his lips. "And I hope you never will," he answered fervently, "so I promise to be on my best behavior and neither ask, beg nor plead. Now get in the bathroom and put those clothes on before I change my mind."

He gave her a little pat on the derriere to move her along, and as Annelise hurried down the hall she knew beyond doubt that, given the chance, Cinderella would have traded Prince Charming in for Rusty Watt any day!

* * * * * *

Silhouette❀Romance

COMING NEXT MONTH

#586 HEART OF GOLD—Sondra Stanford
Melanie Jones, devoted manager of Ettinger's department store, didn't have time for love, but Franklin Harrison Ettinger III was determined to show her that woman does not live by career alone....

#587 THE NEW KID IN TOWN—Stella Bagwell
Widow Natalie Fuller loved coaching her son's Little League baseball team, but her new coaching partner, rugged ex-cowboy Matt Tanner, was more than distracting. Was Natalie falling for the new kid in town?

#588 THE GIFT—Marie Ferrarella
When Eve Tarrington and her kids appeared on Luke Randall's doorstep in a snowstorm, he'd had to offer them shelter. Now he was snowbound with Eve and her family—and the cabin was growing unseasonably warm....

#589 MURPHY'S LAW—Marcine Smith
Farmer Thane MacDougal thought he needed a full-time homemaker for his son, Murphy, but irresistible Meghan Forester—a dedicated veterinarian—was going to shake up his straitlaced notions!

#590 TRUCK DRIVING WOMAN—Elizabeth August
Handsome, wealthy Cole York was way out of truck driver Darcy Raines's league. He'd never be more to her than a self-appointed guardian—or so she thought . . . until he kissed her.

#591 BY HOOK OR BY CROOK—Joan Smith
Shawna Cassidy had become an amateur spy to catch mysterious Kurt Slater stealing her uncle's designs. But by mistake she'd met him . . . and now he was stealing her heart!

AVAILABLE THIS MONTH:

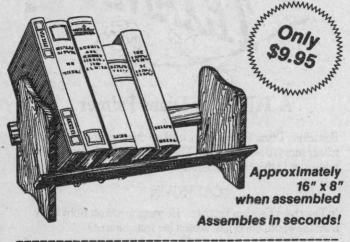

Silhouette Romance

LONG, TALL TEXANS

A Trilogy by Diana Palmer

Bestselling Diana Palmer has rustled up three rugged heroes in a trilogy sure to lasso your heart! The titles of the books are your introduction to these unforgettable men:

CALHOUN

In June, meet Calhoun Ballenger. He wants to protect Abby Clark from the world, but can he protect her from himself?

JUSTIN

Calhoun's brother, Justin—the strong, silent type—has a second chance with the woman of his dreams, Shelby Jacobs, in August.

TYLER

October's long, tall Texan is Shelby's virile brother, Tyler, who teaches shy Nell Regan to trust her instincts—especially when they lead her into his arms!

Don't miss CALHOUN, JUSTIN and TYLER—three gripping new stories coming soon from Silhouette Romance!